Rio Pecos Compound

Rio Pecos Compound

Book Six of
The Clint Mason Series

by

William F. Martin

authorHOUSE®

AuthorHouse™
1663 Liberty Drive
Bloomington, IN 47403
www.authorhouse.com
Phone: 1-800-839-8640

Published by AuthorHouse   12/09/2013

ISBN: 978-1-4918-4133-4 (sc)
ISBN: 978-1-4918-4134-1 (e)

Contents

Chapter 1 1
Chapter 2 16
Chapter 3 29
Chapter 4 42
Chapter 5 50
Chapter 6 56
Chapter 7 63
Chapter 8 70
Chapter 9 84
Chapter 10... 93
Chapter 11.. 103
Chapter 12.. 109
Chapter 13.. 118
Chapter 14.. 128
Chapter 15.. 142
Chapter 16.. 149
Chapter 17.. 158
Chapter 18.. 171
Chapter 19.. 185
Chapter 20 192
Chapter 21.. 203

Chapter 1

Several years had passed since Clint Mason had first ridden into the wide, spreading, grassy valley several days' ride east of Santa Fe. Here the Pecos River, better known as the Rio Pecos, flowed between two steep mountainsides. The mountains formed a natural fence on both sides of the river.

Clint had joined a government survey crew almost five years earlier. The surveyor had been charged with the task of identifying the old Spanish land grants, their boundaries and set markers. The Mexican War had just ended and the United States Government had reached a settlement that gave them ownership of the New Mexico Territory. The U.S. Congress passed various legislation and rulings about the opening of this and other pathways to the West Coast.

The surveyor that Clint was working for back then was a crook, a bully and a lousy gambler. Clint's excellent math and geometry skills advanced him into the confidence of the master surveyor. It also put Clint in a position to see the rip-off the surveyor was pulling on the U.S. Government and land grant holders.

When Clint went to work for this U.S. Government surveyor, Charles Norton, Clint had just turned 20. His six-foot frame was outfitted with a sharp mind, olive skin, dark eyes, wide shoulders and tough as rawhide muscles. It had only been five or six years since he had been driven from his home by a murder frame-up. If anyone had thought Clint was a fast-draw gunman at 15, they would not believe the speed and accuracy that he had developed since. These skills with a gun, even though exceptional, were second rate when compared to his abilities at card playing.

Clint's mathematical mind was tops, and when combined with his ability to read people, he was a gambler without equal. In fact, these exceptional card skills had necessitated the development of the gun skills. During the past five to six years, Clint had been in over 20 gunfights, with only a few scratches or minor holes to show for them. The near-misses had convinced Clint that skill alone was not a guarantee of survival. Using one's head to avoid, or at least to reduce risk, was the answer. Clint's teenage years of hot temper and reckless behavior had given way to deliberate, low-key, and cautious behavior.

Clint had lost too many fights that he should have won, if it had not been for some unforeseen factor. Those memories reminded him of one incident where he had been the hero. A bar fight was raging between a cute little saloon girl and a big drunken miner. The miner was beating the crap out of this girl and no one was stepping in to help. Even though the miner had Clint by at least 100 pounds and had arms twice the size of his, Clint had held the upper hand and was giving the big miner a good beating to teach him a hard lesson. The next thing he knew, the little bit of a woman had crowned him with a bar stool. The miner proceeded to give Clint one of his worst whippings. Who would have thought or predicted that turnaround? That experience and several others had put Clint on a more thoughtful track.

The stamping of the horse under him brought him back out of his memories. He had ridden his horse hard and it was demanding some relief. The vast spread of land before him was his by deed, crook and deception. Down below was some of the best horse flesh that the West had produced. Clint had made it his mission to develop one of the best horse breeds in the country. He had started that dream almost four years ago.

While working for the government surveyor, a large tract of land had been identified between two major Spanish land grants. The survey crew had started calling it the No Man's Land. A few days later, during a rough and tumble card game in a trail town near the Canadian River Basin, things turned deadly. A drifter and gunman caught Norton at cheating. The big, burly drifter had beaten the surveyor almost senseless, then began to pull his bone handled, skinning knife to finish the job.

Clint, without hesitation, shot the drifter and helped his boss through the saloon doors. Norton was begging for his life, when he realized that it was his helper, Clint, who was beside him. Charles Norton, the master surveyor and cheat, promised Clint anything if he would only save him. Norton wanted to get out of the town and far away. It took Norton a week of recovery before he approached Clint about that night at the saloon. Norton expressed his appreciation and thanks for saving his life, but completely overlooked his promise to give Clint anything he wanted. Clint decided to wait for another crisis which he knew would develop. Norton was a bully, a coward, a cheat, and a terrible card player. Sure enough, less than a month later, Norton was again in deep trouble with one of the gambling houses in Santa Fe.

He either had to pay up his gambling debts or a contract would be placed on his head. Norton was aware that Clint always seemed to have cash and he never seemed too lose at cards. Norton wanted Clint to cover his gambling debts so he could settle up with the Santa Fe gambling house. Clint made the deal with the devil. He would bail Norton out of his mess if the surveyor would transfer and record the No Man's Land into Clint's name. Norton protested, saying that the subject tract of land was more than 100,000 acres of top grazing land with water running the entire length. Clint reminded Norton that the land had been stripped from the two Spanish land grants and didn't really belong to Norton. Any resistance drained out of Norton with the realization that Clint had recognized his scheme. The fear of having his gambling debts collected out of his hide persuaded Norton to complete the deal.

Clint could still remember that night in the back room of the Santa Fe gambling house. He had brought a message from Norton and a large cash payment to negotiate the settlement. Clint was wearing his worst trail clothes and he had a few extra gold coins. Four gamblers who saw him could not resist the temptation to fleece the cowboy bumpkin.

A smile crept over Clint's face now, as the sweet memories of how he had cleaned out the house that night many years earlier flooded his mind. Not only did he get the land, but he added to his fortune another major grudge. There had been only two of the four gamblers left standing after that encounter. The group had tried to dry gulch him after the final game. While they had lost the card games, they still were intent on recovering their money and ridding themselves of a trail bum. For Clint's part, when it was all over, the only way he'd be able to return to Santa Fe anytime soon was to become a different person. Thus, a new scheme was needed.

Knowing the type of men he was dealing with, Clint expected an ambush. He knew it would be out of town or in a back alley and without witnesses. The ambush was poorly planned. The gamblers were over-confident about this poorly dressed trail hand. Clint's keen eyes spotted the first two gamblers hiding back in the alley at the rear of the stable. He could guess that they were waiting for him to come for his horse. The other two were probably in the stable or across the alley in a dark doorway where anyone leaving the stable would be an easy target.

Clint's silent, patient surveillance paid off. It was less than 30 minutes before the sparkle of moonlight on a gun barrel in the darkened doorway gave the dry gulcher away. Clint put two shots into the dark opening, producing a terrible howl. A second round of shots honed-in on the orange flashes that the two alley gamblers were blindly sending his way. One of the gamblers stumbled forward and collapsed. Everything went quiet for a moment. Then, two horses raced out the other end of the alley.

Clint eased himself back into the shadows and casually strolled to the nearest café. He looked like a typical drifter or range hand, eating a late meal. No one would have guessed he had just walked away from a deadly gun battle that left two men dead. It was not long before some excited customers brought the story to the café. Clint listened with typical curiosity, as a spectator.

Clint had then returned to his domain with a master plan. While 100,000 acres was not the biggest of spreads in this territory, the quality of those acres, plus the water, made up for the difference. His hopes were high. This could be the end of roaming the west and constantly running into trouble. The New Mexico Territory was almost without law and order. The Spaniards had been driven back to Mexico. The Pueblos, Navajo and Apache Indians had been harassed, cheated and confined. They were restless and beginning to fight back. The eastern settlers were starting to move on the land. Gold and silver had been discovered north of that area and also in California. This discovery of gold was like a magnet, pulling the worst of mankind. If this was not enough, the Mexican War had left a lot of Mexicans and U.S. misfit soldiers, deserters and criminals in the region.

The U.S. Government had sent soldiers to Santa Fe to provide some law and order. Their orders to keep the peace were not easy to obey. The government quarters in Santa Fe was a makeshift building, and the commander could not control his men in rough and tumble Santa Fe. The gambling, drinking, corruption and graft were out of control.

Into this mess rode a man with the courage and will power to fight against the odds. Clint was a gambler by heart and by trade.

He gazed over his land with a sense of pride and accomplishment. He was not a nobleman from Spain who had been given vast amounts of land. Nor was he a rich land buyer from the east that came west with his vast amounts of wealth. He was a drifter, gambler, gunman, and a sought-after fugitive, but he had used his skill and tenacity to acquire this beautiful land. It wasn't a ranch yet, but it would be someday.

Clint pulled a spyglass from his saddlebag. He was trying to locate the old adobe house that had been built on that land years ago. Shortly after acquiring the tract of land, Clint had brought in a few horses. He had spent some time patching the roof of the old Spanish adobe ranch house, cleaning out the hand-dug well and repairing the fireplace. The adobe structure was probably over 200 years old, but in excellent structural shape. Those southwestern adobe houses could last almost forever if the roof was maintained and the caps of the walls maintained by replacing the mud loss due to rain and wind.

A faint column of smoke brought his spyglass to rest on the ranch house. He could see the top of the building and its chimney, but no smoke. As he passed a little to the right, he saw that the smoke was coming from a Navajo-style mud hut.

Anyone watching the bronze-colored face of this stoic rider would never have detected a single change of expression. Clint's poker face had been trained by hundreds of card games and gun fights to give no clue about the rage, excitement or concern flowing in his veins. The prospect that someone had moved onto his land would have thrown most men into a rage, prompting a direct confrontation to stir the trespassers up and out immediately.

Since he had been away almost two years, he decided on taking a few hours or days to investigate. Clint surprised even himself seeing how patience and caution had replaced his youthful recklessness. Near-death experiences have a way of providing some wisdom. At the very least, these near-misses help a person to establish priorities for life.

A few hours of observation provided a reasonable explanation for the activities he had observed. The people looked to be Navajo women and children. He could see some sheep nearby and what looked like a wool table and some weaving frames. It would appear that some Navajos had moved onto the ranch and set up a camp near the ranch house and well. Clint had seen many of these camps up north in Navajo country, but never this far south. This region was more likely to be the hunting grounds of the Apache. No one seemed to go near his ranch house. Clint had been on the trail for two weeks and that ranch house looked very inviting. He decided to move on down to the Navajo camp and his ranch house well before dark. If he came in slowly, maybe he wouldn't get shot at out of fear.

He knew a few Navajo greeting words that would help, he hoped. He was also leading two other horses that would make him appear to be a ranch hand or worker. A few Navajo greetings or hellos to the camp were finally responded to with a greeting from an older woman near one of the mud huts. It only took a few moments for the verbal exchange to switch to Spanish. Both he and the woman were fluent, and that served a lot better than his limited Navajo.

The history of the Navajo group that was moving onto the ranch was soon explained. They had been raided several times up north by white buffalo hunters, their wool stolen, some sheep slaughtered and most of their range camps destroyed. Word had gotten around that the grazing was a lot better south of Raton Pass, but that rumor had missed the detail that it was fierce Apache land. As they moved onto the large grassy plateau south of Raton Pass, the Apache raided them several times, taking their wool blankets, meat and supplies. The Navajo group then continued to move south, crossing over the divide into the high plain of the Rio Pecos. Last winter they had come upon this vacant ranch. The well was good, shelter was available and no one seemed to be around. The condition of the corrals and ranch house indicated that this ranch owner would return. They decided to settle until that happened, and take advantage of the fertile, under-used valley.

Since arriving near the ranch, they had not been attacked. The Navajos were interested in staying nearby and would gladly pay or trade for the privilege. Clint assured them that they could stay if a fair arrangement was worked out. The ranch was going to be built up with horses, sheep and cattle. The Navajos acknowledged that they had found the herd of horses up in a dead end canyon just west of the ranch. They had recognized the high quality of the horses, and the discovery had confirmed their suspicions that they were on an occupied ranch.

An agreement was reached: The Navajo could continue to herd their sheep here, live in their huts and weave their blankets. In exchange for this privilege, they would care for the ranch house, herd Clint's sheep with theirs, and give the ranch one-half of all lambs born to the Navajo herd. In addition to the sheep herding, they would care for the horses in Rock Canyon. The ranch would provide protection for the Navajos and their sheep. Clint also offered to assist them when trading trips were needed to buy supplies and sell wool, meat and blankets.

This arrangement seemed to please the Navajos. The Navajo shepherds would be a good way for Clint to build his sheep herd. It would also discourage drifters and vandals when they could see the ranch was occupied.

It was late when Clint left the Navajo campfire. He was looking forward to a good night's rest under the roof of his own house. A couple of the women had been cleaning the house and building a kitchen fire inside as the bargaining had dragged on around the campfire. Clint had brought a little rye whiskey to the meeting. It was just enough to ease the tension and increase the openness.

With everyone in final agreement, Clint had withdrawn to his clean adobe dwelling. The Navajos had even placed some very thick wool blankets on the wood frame bed. He slept like a newborn puppy.

Over the next few days, Clint worked with a couple of the Navajo boys to repair the canyon fences that held the horses. The large pasture in this canyon could hold a lot more horses without over grazing. The spring-fed basin at the upper end of the canyon provided more than enough water for a herd three times the number that Clint had gathered so far. Clint spent some time breaking in new mounts and retraining at least three of the horses which Clint had brought here two years ago. They had been saddle-wise when he left them, but freedom gives horses a strong will to challenge the master with. Luckily, it only takes a little firm control to bring their memories back.

It was time to put Clint's plan into motion. The house was in good order, the horses were secure and retrained, and the Navajos were going about sheep herding and blanket-making as they had done for over 100 years. The Navajo women amazed him. They were completely self-sufficient if left to live in peace. They demanded and expected nothing. They only wanted to be left alone to live their nomadic lifestyle.

This ranch provided the complete habitat for the sheep and the Navajo – the upper range of the mountains in the summer, then the low lying protected grass lands during the winter. The Indians had built several hut camps along the sheep trails from mountain range to valley. These people moved smoothly from camp to camp as the sheep moved along. The elderly women stayed in the base camp or permanent camp with the smallest children and did most of the weaving on bigger looms. The young girls did most of the herding. The young boys did not seem to be expected to herd, and Clint thought that perhaps that was because they weren't very good at it. The Navajo men were few and far between. The two older men in the group seemed only to work on making silver jewelry and to go away on trading trips for long periods of time. They never asked for protection and were often gone for weeks.

Part of Clint's plan was to build up a large sheep herd. The market was good for wool, mutton and blankets. Clint had learned a lot about developing sheep herds. The Churro breed was well suited for this climate and terrain, but produced poor quality wool and in small amounts. However, the mutton off the bare-belly, ugly little critter was excellent. The Merino sheep with its thicker, tighter wool could be crossbred with the Churro sheep. Watching the development was important because the Merino was not as hardy and did not proliferate as rapidly as the Churro. A good breeder aims to tease the best of both sheep strains into a better animal.

The Navajos did not like some of the finer, fuzzier wools of the Merino, preferring the longer coarse hair of the Churro. However, Clint had noticed that they were very adept at using both wool types. The blankets he saw around the huts were beautiful, and Clint knew immediately that they would trade for top dollar.

It was time for Clint to make a trip into Santa Fe. The Navajos wanted to make a trading trip to sell blankets and mutton so they could buy supplies – and also two Navajo men had prepared some jewelry for sale. They needed more silver and turquoise to tool new jewelry.

The ground rules Clint suggested provided the Navajos some protection from a safe distance.

To do this, he planned to disguise himself as a Mexican hide-trader. He would travel separately, but within range to protect them against bandits and thugs. When they got to Santa Fe, they would not acknowledge each other. They would spend no more than three days at the Santa Fe market. If able to complete their trading earlier, they would leave. Clint would watch and follow them every step of the way.

The three-day trip into Santa Fe went without a hitch. The trading went very well and the blankets and silver jewelry were purchased quickly. By the second afternoon, the supplies were mostly purchased and loaded onto the wagons. The plan was to finish the trading the following morning and get an early start back to Rio Pecos. The camping area for traders was just south of the main market plaza. Clint knew that watchful eyes would have noticed the good trades this band of Navajos was making. Thus, he had increased his vigilance anticipating some attack.

The Navajos had settled in for the night when Clint's watchful eye spotted four men sneaking up on their wagons. The lead man was climbing up onto one wagon when he put out a groan, jerked awkwardly to one side and fell back. One of the other would-be robbers crawled up to his partner and turned him over. Protruding from his fellow partner's chest was the wicked end of an arrow. Quietly, he drew back to the third man and they started sneaking away. When they got back to their horses, their fourth member was laying on the ground in a pool of blood. Two of their best horses were missing, along with all their gear.

The two surviving bandits rode off at top speed into the night.

The Navajo trading party returned to the marketplace the next morning without being aware of the night's near robbery and killings. There was no trace of bodies or horses. They heard rumors around the trading tables about the bodies of two troublemakers that had been found in a dry wash outside of town. Murder was so common that not much was made of it. The wagons were loaded and the return trip to Rio Pecos was completed without incident. As far as the Navajos knew, the trip was without problems. They never saw Clint during the entire time. Two extra horses were tied to their wagons sometime during the return trip.

Clint was not seen for several days. However, the housekeeper reported to the other Navajos that a strange looking bow and some arrows were hanging in the back mud room of the ranch house. The Spaniard cross bow was not a common weapon in this territory. If the Indians had known European history, they would have recognized that the deadly devices dated back to the conflicts between the Moors and the Christians in Spain more than 500 years earlier.

Clint had been busy in Santa Fe during the trading trip. He had contacted the Santa Fe banker who had been handling his money for the previous ten years. The banker knew him as Cliff Martinez, a rancher and representative of Brad Mason, a banker and rancher from Manatee County, in the southern part of New Mexico Territory. The banker, Mr. James Jenson, was unaware that Brad Mason and Clint were brothers. Brad,

Clint's older brother, was not actually involved in any of these financial dealings. Clint had used his brother's name so that if anything was to happen to Clint, then the considerable funds he had raised would go to Brad. Clint was a fugitive from the law in Manatee County, while Brad was a well-respected rancher and banker.

Clint had to perform a vanishing act in Santa Fe during the trading trip. His disguise as a Mexican hide-trader had to be switched to that of a clean-cut rancher for the banker, and then back into the dirty hide-trader gear.

Clint had chosen a stable on one of Santa Fe's back alleys for this transition of identities. The stable was run by a giant black man. The blacksmith who went by the name of Joe Black did not ask questions and was willing to rent Clint a small room in the stable hay loft. Mr. Black was more than willing to clean out the small room for the handsome rent Clint offered. This stable hideaway was just right for his dealings, allowing him to move by foot in and out of the side streets, cafés and saloons without raising any curiosity from on-lookers. The side door of the stable led directly to the loft ladder. Clint could go and come without disturbing Mr. Black, who had his living quarters attached to the other side of the large stable building.

Chapter 2

The last trip to Santa Fe had been quite rewarding. His Navajo herders were well supplied with favorable trades for their jewelry, wool, blankets and mutton. Clint was able to reactivate his financial ties to Mr. Jenson, the Santa Fe banker. Also, a surprising piece of information that Clint had picked up at the card tables involved a possible source for a large sheep herd.

Clint had returned to the Santa Fe gambling tables after having escorted the Navajos back to his Rio Pecos Compound. Clint's finances were in great shape, but extra cash was always useful. He enjoyed matching wits with gamblers, but mostly he was gathering information. Clint's Mexican hide-trader image proved to be an excellent cover. The gamblers could accept that this hide-trader would have money, and was a reasonably smart trader, but their confidence was high that they were smarter than any lowly Mexican.

The tale gradually developed that cattlemen were moving their herds on to the high plains of northern Texas. The Spanish and Mexican land holders of that region were no match for the gunmen that the cattle owners were hiring from Texas and the East. A range war was brewing.

A myth was spreading that sheep and cattle could not share the same range. The truth was that the smell of sheep was offensive to the cattlemen. The cattlemen spread the rumor that the oil from the sheep hoofs was poisoning the soil. The U.S. Congress was promoting the expansion westward. Beef was much more acceptable to eastern markets than mutton.

The stories around the gambling tables in Santa Fe told of sheep drives of more than 100,000 sheep being stopped by Texas rustlers. It was no secret that the emerging cattle barons were behind those raids. The stories hinted at the prospect that thousands of sheep could be purchased for pennies per head. The Spanish land holders had Basque herders that tended the sheep. But, they were shepherds and not gunmen. A shepherd on foot was no match for a mounted gunman. The huge landholdings of the sheep owners were being overrun by the migrating wave of cattle from the east. Many of the large Spanish land grant holders were going broke. They had originally been supported by almost limitless wealth from Spain. When Spain and Mexico split, the U.S. and Mexican War had stopped the flows of money and support. The major market for wool, mutton and sheep was Mexico, and the cattlemen were blocking that passageway. So, the sheep owners were being starved without a way to sell their product.

Clint had learned enough about sheep history to know that some very large sheep trail drives had been made from Texas into New Mexico Territory more than 100 years earlier. The Spanish had also brought sheep overland from California. The animals had flourished so well in the Rio Grande Valley that the Spanish grant holders had moved hundreds of thousands of them down the

Rio Grande valley to Mexico for sale. So the trail drive from the Texas high plains to the Rio Pecos Compound was possible. It would take at least 50 herders, plus dogs and pack horses to make the drive. While the Navajo women were excellent sheep herders, they were not suited for that kind of drive.

Clint decided to head to Texas with only a string of horses and a set of saddlebags filled with gold. He looked forward to the open range ride and the solitude. He loved this country; wild sage, hawks overhead, flowering cactus, and great horses under saddle. The outdoors living could always be accented with occasional visits to trail town saloons.

He loved the outdoor solitude, but a challenging game of chance with shrewd card sharks was even more stimulating. There was always that adrenaline rush when tempers flared and gun play could be split-seconds away. Very few card games ended with pistols drawn, but the threat was always there. The more likely outcome was being bushwhacked in some dark alley after a victory.

It took less than two weeks of steady riding to reach the Texas high plains. Clint rode into the midst of a sheep herd that stretched almost as far as he could see. The shepherds were leery, but directed him to a giant Spanish hacienda in a wooded grove near some small rolling hills. Additional Spanish adobe buildings covered several acres. The whole place was protected by heavily armed Mexican gunmen. The buildings and adobe walls formed a fort-like setting.

Clint was invited into a lavish sitting room. The furnishings must have cost a fortune just to ship there from Spain and Mexico City. It was some time before anyone came to greet him, but he was busy entertaining himself by examining the wall hangings and especially a display of old weapons. He spotted a cross-bow that was almost identical to the one he had just used on that robber in Santa Fe.

After a considerable delay, a tall, very dignified, gray-haired Spanish man approached him through one of the big arches. The tile work on the walls and entrance arches was beautiful. Each doorway was a piece of art. The elderly gentleman named Juan Martinez introduced himself as the owner and welcomed Clint to his home. While Clint was touring the Martinez art collection, Sr. Martinez was examining his mounts. The gentleman was quick to express his admiration for Clint's fine string of horses.

It did not take Clint long to get through the formalities of greetings and bring up the purpose of his visit: He was there to buy sheep. The word up north was that the Texas cattlemen were trying to take over the range and drive the sheep off. It was also rumored that a superior line of sheep had been developed in this area of Texas by cross-breeding the Churro and Merino.

The Spanish patriarch was noticeably impressed that this rough-looking fellow would even be aware of such developments. Clint was asked to join the table for the evening meal. They would then discuss business later over drinks.

The dinner was excellent and lavish. Music was provided and beautiful young women kept the wine glasses full. The imported wine was outstanding and no doubt expensive. It occurred to Clint that he was being impressed with the grandeur and open display of wealth. This was probably to counter the rumor that the Texans were bankrupting the wealthy Spanish families. It could also be the lead-in to hard bargaining for the price of sheep. If it could be established that the sale of sheep was not needed or urgent, it would put Sr. Martinez in a better bargaining position.

After a rambling discussion of taxes, Mexican war, sheep breeding and the furnishings in his hacienda, the bargaining for the sheep herd was begun. Sr. Martinez was definitely impressed and pleased that Clint was interested in 100,000 head of sheep. That was the size of his remaining herd. Martinez had seen the cattlemen overrunning other sheep ranches so he had started a few years ago developing his own cattle herd. On occasion, his Basque sheepherders had been harassed, threatened and some were killed. It was then revealed that Sr. Martinez owned only 80% of these sheep. The Basque herders were partial owners and were working on a percentage of each lamb crop.

The Basque were a proud people and worked independently of the Spanish landlord. Both the sheep and the Basque herders had been brought to this country by the Spanish government. The business arrangement had always been a mutual shared partnership between landowner and shepherd.

These sheep herders followed the same lifestyle that existed for them over 1,000 years earlier in

Spain and Eastern Europe. It was most likely that the Great Hannibal had encountered the Basque sheepherders 200 years before Christ.

A tentative agreement was reached pending the concurrence of the Basque. Sr. Juan Martinez would accept 100 pounds of coin for his interest in the sheep herd. Martinez was sure the Basque herders would be more than willing to join Clint in a new partnership. Martinez had discussed on several occasions the Basques' desire to move toward the New Mexico Territory. The Texas raiders had killed so many herders and sheep with the raids becoming more and more frequent and ruthless.

A meeting would be arranged for Clint to present his proposal to the Basque herders. This clan of herders included more than 30 men, women and children. Clint cooled his heels for two days waiting for this meeting. The days were pleasant and relaxing and the accommodations were the best he had ever experienced. These Spanish landowners knew how to live. The guest suite he was provided was plush and spacious. Together with the excellent wine being served at every meal, the feather bed was so inviting that he was having trouble keeping his early-to-rise habit. Beautiful, young, dark-eyed girls were everywhere, waiting on tables, bringing clean towels, offering to do laundry, and cleaning this huge hacienda. Life was so good here Clint wondered why he was feeling the restless urge to get back onto the trail.

The meeting with the herders went very well. They were interested in leaving this hostile area. The rumors had also reached them over the past several years that the New Mexico Territory was an excellent habitat for the sheep. If they could keep the same ownership relationship, 20-percent of livestock and 20-percent of all lambs, wool, and mutton, they were ready to move immediately. Protection from the cattlemen was their major concern. Moving the sheep herd the long distance to Rio Pecos valley was no big deal. They were nomadic people, so moving with the herd was their normal day-to-day style of living. Their ancestors going back for hundreds of years had herded sheep all over Europe before they were brought to Mexico.

The drive northwest into the New Mexico Territory would be similar to their everyday activities. The head of the Basque herders assured Clint that his clan could handle the entire herd without assistance as long as bandits did not cause problems.

Sr. Martinez offered a partial solution. Eight of his young Mexican guards were interested in making the trip up toward Santa Fe. In exchange for food, fresh mounts and minimal expenses, they would ride guard for the herd. As soon as Clint had purchased some additional horses from Martinez, the drive was underway.

Clint had provided a trail map to the guards and the shepherds. However, the Basque herders let Clint know that they were quite aware of the best route to the Rio Pecos basin. They had already been planning to take their 20 percent of the herd to that region if Sr. Martinez could not provide the needed protection. The best way to get from this northwestern area of Texas into the northern portion of the Rio Pecos was through the

Canadian River Passageway in the New Mexico Territory.

The Basque herders would follow the Canadian River west and then slightly northwest into the Mora Spanish land grant area. This route would bring them to the Santa Fe Trail on a high plateau just south of the Raton Pass. The sheep could then be moved along southwest, parallel to the Santa Fe Trail, until they hit the Rio Pecos. The map that ex-surveyor Clint gave the Basque leader was well landmarked and detailed. It was anticipated the drive would take two months if all went without a hitch. The young Mexican guards were biting at the bit. They were looking forward to the trip. The slow movement with the shepherd was something they could tolerate for a couple of months. After all they had been working beside the Basque for several years and they liked the food they provided. The Basque seemed to make a great camp every night. Life on the trail was just a way of life for these herders. They always seemed to be at home whenever they stopped. The Mexican guards had also been provided the best mounts that Sr. Martinez would sell. As the new owner, Clint was supplementing their riding stock with the loan of his horses. None of these Mexican riders had ever ridden on such powerful and enduring horses. This was going to be a great adventure, although Clint was a little concerned with the eagerness of the young Mexican gun hands.

A trial drive could turn ugly and treacherous at a single bend in the river. He urged all the caution these young heads would take, and then the drive was underway.

Juan Martinez suggested that maybe the cattlemen would support the removal of sheep from this range. This gave Clint the idea to try the idea on a few of the largest cattlemen in the area. The trail town of Amarillo was only a day's hard ride southeast. Martinez suggested the Golden Nugget Saloon and Hotel as a good contact place, and offered the name of Major Henry Bell as a good starting place if Clint was interested in knowing who was behind most of the raids against Martinez's herds. This connection had not been proven, nor would the governor-appointed marshal even look into the problem. Amarillo was a cattle town. It was also a wide open free-for-all frontier outpost. It seemed the worst of the east was moving west in search of riches. Many of these gamblers, ex-soldiers and get-rich-quick business people had made it to Amarillo.

The challenge was giving Clint a rush that he would have to control. He was beginning to feel the same as some of these young Mexican guards that were headed to Santa Fe with his herd.

The fresh air and open range was giving him a lift. It was surprising in that he was leaving the luxury of a big Spanish hacienda with soft beds and beautiful maids to sleep under the stars out in the open. There had to be a little insanity in his family tree. As he headed southeast toward Amarillo, the cattle herds became more numerous and sheep were much less noticeable. Clint had taken his time so he would arrive at the gambling tables late evening the next day.

The town looked as Sr. Martinez had described: rough, big saloons, lots of cowboys, much glitter and frenzy. The Golden Nugget could not be missed with its gaudy lanterns, painted signs, large hitching rail and covered porch along the entire front face. The clink of piano and raucous singing could be heard almost a block away. Juan Martinez had given Clint a drawing of a number of the largest outfit brands so he could recognize the horses and thus their riders. Major Henry Bell's brand was a Circle B, and that brand was on several horses outside the Golden Nugget. It was Clint's bet that the big white stallion with silver-trimmed black saddle belonged to Major Bell. No working cowboy would have such a show horse. A close look at the big white stallion revealed a lot about Major Bell, in particular the spur marks and sore mouth told of a cruel and over-controlling master. Clint tried not to let emotion interfere with business, but the mistreatment of animals did raise his boiling point.

It only took a minute inside the saloon to spot the arrogant Major. He was surrounded by people catering to him. The king was definitely lording over his domain. A direct entrance into the card game with the Major was highly unlikely. An indirect approach would have to be developed.

After moving around the saloon for over an hour, a table was chosen where two or three of the five men were from Circle B Ranch. Clint had overheard some talk at the table that identified the cowboys. When one of the players eventually excused himself, Clint asked if he could join the game.

This card game was slow-paced and friendly; none of these men were much into hard gambling. It didn't take long for the topic of sheep to enter the discussion. The men shared the undesirable job of driving the sheep off the open range. The cowboys all complained about the messy job. The sheep could not be stampeded like cattle. The little wooly critters would just scatter and then stand there. When you would pull back, the sheep would come back together. Even shooting some of them didn't drive the others away. Besides, the dead carcasses on the range only stunk up the place, and the cattle won't come near a sheep carcass.

The cowboys were also reporting that Major Bell was getting very impatient with them. You could tell these cowboys didn't like their job. They had been brought here with the cattle herds. They liked the cowboy life and didn't want anything to do with shepherding.

Clint worked into the conversation the fact that he knew some people that would drive those sheep off the open range. The cowboys were very interested and they were sure their boss would pay good money to have the sheep gone. Major Bell had a lot of his men tied up with the on-going sheep problem. Besides, the sheep also ruined the open range grass for the cattle. Those sheep stunk up the grazing area for miles. Major Bell had also told his ranch hands that sheep could spread disease to the cattle and people.

It didn't take long after Clint's card game had broken up that an invite arrived to join Major Bell for drinks. The Major was a shrewd business man as well as an arrogant cattleman. The idea that the sheep problem could be solved immediately was worth a lot to him. The illegal operation he was funding to drive the sheep ranchers off the range or to break them was costing him a lot of money and time. If Clint could do this job within one week, Major Bell would be willing to pay up to one cent per head for each sheep removed. Clint countered the offer with two cents per head. He agreed that he would remove 100,000 sheep off the Texas high plateau within five days.

With an advance of 50 $20 gold coins as a binder, the balance of the gold coin payment could be made at the northwest corner of Major Bell's desired open range when all the sheep were gone. This deal Major Bell was more than willing to accept. If this operation was successful, he would save more than the two cents per sheep head in manpower and lost cattle grazing fat. He knew that the cowboys did not like the killing of sheep and that they had not been successful in driving the animals off the range.

He also knew that Sr. Martinez, the largest sheep ranch owner, had recently hired some Mexican gunmen or guards that were making the raids more risky and more difficult.

Major Bell handed over the 50 gold coins and the deal was set in motion. Clint told the major he would start his men moving tonight. He was a little worried that some of Major Bell's range hands might spot the sheep herd that was already moving west off the open range.

If Major Bell had that information, it could make it rather difficult to collect the balance of the gold payment. Clint's sneaky plan might not produce the windfall profit that he anticipated. Even so, the pure fun of it was worth a lot of gold to his soul. As Clint rode out of town with his pockets full of gold coins, he could not hold back the laughter and shouts of joy.

The next four days were spent making fresh track over the sheep trail his herd had left almost a week earlier. The Basque herders had made good time. The round-up had been completed. There was not a single sheep to be seen anywhere. The fifth day brought four Circle B cowboys approaching his position, just as the agreement plan had specified. Clint had chosen a small rock outcrop with a few trees for cover right at the edge of a big grassy plateau drop off. The land west of here became very rough, very quickly. The transfer of this amount of money could be dangerous. Most of the cowboys would not see that much gold in their lifetime. Greed can do a lot to a man's mind, so Clint had taken some precautions.

As the cowboys drew near, Clint moved into the opening near the campfire. He had gathered three of his spare horses which were staked out near the trees behind him. Clint wanted these cowboys to worry about what could be hidden behind the rock outcrop and in the trees. Clint would never know if his bluff worked or the cowboys decided to be fair and square and to pay up on the contract. The deal was completed. The four cowboys rode away, back toward Major Bell's spread. Clint packed his gold on one of those spare horses and followed his herd's trail west into New Mexico Territory.

Chapter 3

Almost three weeks had passed since Clint had purchased the sheep herd from Sr. Juan Martinez. The Basque herders had made excellent time moving the 100,000 head of sheep. He noticed that the trail was getting very fresh, so the herd could not be very far in front of him.

Then he saw one of his horses he had left with the Mexican guards lying dead in a wash. The alarm shot through his body; instant keen alertness. He used the spyglass to scan the trail. He noticed a few white clumps in the distance and soon learned that they were dead sheep. Reading the tracks told the story of five or six bandits that had raided the Basque camp. However, the Basque carts and sheep trail continued. It would appear the bandits pulled out without success and had headed south. Clint knew that the trail they'd taken led toward the town of Tucumcari.

Within a few hours of hard riding, Clint came upon the sheep herd. The Mexican guards met him at the rear of the herd. Once they recognized him, he was waved on in. The Basque had already set up camp for the night, but everyone was on high alert for another attack. They were sure glad to see a friendly face and another gun hand.

The story they told about the raid was short. The only person hurt was one of the young Mexican guards. The bandits apparently had not realized the sheepherders had an armed guard unit with them. The bandits had ridden into their camp last night demanding money, food and horses while the Mexican guards had been out front of the herd scouting the next day's drive. When they came back into camp, the surprised bandits started shooting wildly. The bandits had then dropped everything and rode at a dead run back down the riverbed. A stray bullet had hit one of the guard's horses. The tumble had killed the horse and hurt the Mexican rider. The rider's injury was not serious, but the Basque shepherds had suggested an early camp just in case. They would not be able to outrun the bandits, so a well-fortified camp would be their best chance and their injured guard could rest up a couple of days. If the bandits did not come back, the trail drive could then continue. This would also give them the opportunity to go back and dress out the two or three sheep that had been killed.

The injured guard had some bruises and scrapes, plus a sprained ankle, but the biggest injury was to his pride. The other young gunmen were ready and anxious to track down the bandits. Clint finally calmed them down. The drive would continue. Clint and one guard would follow the bandits' tracks. His earlier scouting had convinced him that the gang was headed to Tucumcari. They were either going for help or maybe they had decided that trying to rob a guarded sheep camp wasn't worth the risk. The camp needed a few supplies, so one guard and Clint would trail the bandits. If that led them to a trading post, they could stock up. If the bandits were getting help, then the warning could quickly be brought back to the herd.

Clint's guess turned out to be accurate. The bandits' tracks lead straight to the town of Tucumcari. When the guard pointed out two riders that had raided the sheep camp, Clint sent the guard to the general store to buy the supplies they needed. A trip to the saloon and café would probably let him know if the bandits were organizing another raid. It didn't take Clint long to learn that these riders were not interested in any sheep herd that had armed guards. It turned out that two of the raiders had been hurt . . . one fairly seriously. These Mexican young guns must be pretty good shots to hit two of the hard riding bandits.

When Clint and the guard got back to the old campsite, the herd had moved on. These Basque knew their business. Herding sheep was both a process and a way of life. The sheep grazed on the move, so a slow-moving herd was better fed than one that was stationery. Clint could also tell that the entire Basque clan was starting to push. They were anxious to get to the new ranch.

They were still following the Canadian River west by northwest, a path that would take them through the big Mora land grant. The western edge of the Mora Spanish land grant would butt up against the Santa Fe Trail. Clint knew the area pretty well from his land surveying days. The Mora Range covered the headwaters of the Canadian River and the high plains that served as a divide to the Rio Pecos drainage basin.

Once they cleared the steep mountain range on their left, the herd could be turned south.

The large grass range looked like a giant smooth dome between two rivers. The grass and sage was swaying in the breeze like silk sheets. The mountains had been eroded down between the two rivers and formed a natural passageway. Early explorers and native Indians had discovered this route long before the Santa Fe Trail was named.

The Basque shepherds realized that their old stories about this route were being confirmed. Some earlier Basque herders had been brought up the Rio Grande almost 200 years ago by the Spanish Army.

Clint was rather confident that his herd had been on the Mora Grant for at least two days. A challenge by some Mora riders was expected. Holding and protecting your land was mostly done by force rather than by law. The Mora family was not objecting to the passage of his herd, they just wanted to make sure everyone understood the rules. The accepted practice was open range to move herds, but ownership of the land was fiercely defended. There was only a brief encounter with the Mora riders, who observed the herd from a distance. Two more hard days passed before the front scouts brought word about the upcoming Santa Fe Trail.

A prolonged discussion with the herders and Mexican guards around the campfire that night led to a consensus. The main sheep herd would move slowly over the divide between the Rio Pecos and the Canadian, and then keep east of the Santa Fe Trail and head south. The families, carts and some guards would take the much easier path by using the main trail. At this point, they were only a few days from the Rio Pecos Compound. The herders would use a light camp tonight and meet for one last major camp setup before making the final push onto the Rio Pecos Compound land.

After the herd had crested the divide, stray sheep began to join the herd. Scattered bunches of ten, 20 and 30 sheep were found wandering the brush at the edges of the grass plain. Occasionally, the sheep would have a tattoo brand, but mostly they were unmarked. Most of the strays were in bad shape, often with injuries that needed tending. If the sheep were too far gone, they would be slaughtered for their hides and meat. The Basque herders were very skilled at saving sheep, but the whole process did slow the march south.

Clint and four of the guards stayed with the families and carts on the Santa Fe Trail. The other four guards watched after the shepherds. Moving the horses through the floodplain area with the sheep herd was slow and difficult on the mounts. The brush and cactus could rip the hide of a horse if great care wasn't taken. But the wooly sheep seemed to be at home in the underbrush along the Rio Pecos. The map that Clint had drawn gave the shepherds clear landmarks to follow. The carts and everyone else would proceed to set up a good campsite two days' drive south.

It was possible that the procession of carts, horses and people headed down the Santa Fe Trail could invite ambush. The trail was a lucrative source of supplies for the lazy, the unemployed and the thugs. The Mexican guards were cautioned over and over again about the risks on this well-traveled trail. While show of force may keep the small bands of thieves at bay, the presence of excellent horses, loaded carts and families might entice a larger bandit group to attack.

The first night's camp just off the Santa Fe Trail gave Clint a chance to night scout the land south of him. The guards would take turns with the patrol duties. It was emphasized that everyone and the animals needed to stay rested so that an emergency drive could be made if conditions dictated. The camp was to move on south the next morning. Clint's scouting trip turned up a campfire back in the hills west of the trail. The moonlight was just bright enough for Clint to get in close. The group of men gathered around the fire numbered close to a dozen. The guns, mounts and clothes of these men indicated that they were rustlers. Although Clint could not hear the conversation, it was clear they were planning a raid. Their gestures and pointing led Clint to believe his caravan was the most likely target. He moved around the perimeter of the camp until he located the horses. He counted fourteen riding horses and two pack mules with only one guard on duty. Bandits often did not take precautions to guard themselves. In their minds, they were the aggressors who would do the attacking.

There was no way of knowing for sure the intent of these men, but some prevention was in order. Clint was able to sneak around and disable the dozing guard. The horses and mules were then turned loose. Four of the best horses were led away, knowing that most of the other horses would follow. If Clint could steal their mounts, it might take these potential rustlers a couple of days to reorganize. Most of the horses were saddled, which was another clue that this was a group of bandits. Ranchers, travelers and honest people didn't leave their horses saddled all night. Without saddles and their best mounts, they would not be able to muster a raid. If this group turned out to be innocent, they just run into some bad luck. The only injury was a bump on the head of the lonely guard. Clint had also wasted a little of his whisky with a splash on the gent's clothes. Hopefully, his comrades would blame him for getting drunk and falling off his perch.

When Clint was a good distance from the campfire, he hooked a big brush and dragged it along behind to cover his tracks. The other loose horses were wandering along in a random path, but in general following his direction. Once he had intersected the Santa Fe Trail, the track would be masked by all the other travelers. Clint headed to the next designated camp location where he could rest and wait for the caravan to reach him. He had put in a good night's work and sleep was beckoning him.

It was late the next afternoon before the Basque caravan with the Mexican guards found his campsite. He had spent the afternoon cleaning the area, building a nice fireplace, and dragging in some dry firewood. The stolen horses had all been unsaddled and their gear hidden. The horses were then driven further south and down toward the waterholes that were near the river. The better grazing and the water should keep the horses off the high and dry Santa Fe Trail. These riders had had some very good riding stock. If Clint could ever find out the intent of those riders, he could either let them find their own horses or he could come back and retrieve the best for his own ranch.

The pack mules finally wandered into camp with their packs still on. These poor animals were probably looking for someone to remove their burden. A thorough inspection of the mule packs convinced Clint that the owners were indeed bandits. The packs were full of guns, jewelry, copper pots and pans, and anything of value that these bandits had collected from various travelers.

The variety of jewelry indicated several different families had been robbed. Knowing that most people could identify their own jewelry, Clint had the idea to display these family heirlooms on the Santa Fe square. True, it might be a little tricky to avoid being charged with the robbery, so he would have to devise a plan. He couldn't help thinking of the joy that would spread across a poor settler's face upon retrieving a family locket or other keepsake. Most of the westward moving families had given up almost everything for this move. They would often bring small pieces of their family history with them just to maintain some connection with their past. When those few pieces are stolen, the hurt and anger can stay with you for years. There was some risk in keeping the loot in his possession, but Clint wanted to attempt to return these items to their owners. Everything was placed in the carts under the hides and wool. The mules were then stripped of their packs and turned loose.

Clint rotated the guards all night. He did not want to be surprised. But, without event, the next morning saw the caravan heading south. If all went smoothly, there would be one more major campsite on the trail, then a long day's drive into the Rio Pecos Compound.

This upcoming last night on the trail would be a good time to celebrate. The Basque herders would not be far away with the flock, so most of these men could be brought into the camp for the night. One of the guards was sent back to check on the progress of the herd. The distance between the caravan and the herd was a little greater than Clint had expected, so it was decided by the women of the caravan to stop early so the herd and their men could catch up. Clint had to be reminded that herding sheep was their way of life. Camping on the trail was their home. One more day to the ranch was not a big thing for them.

Even though the camp had been set up about mid-afternoon, it was almost sunset before everyone finally gathered around the feast. The women had gone all out to make a huge meal. The sky was a golden orange with streaks of a pure gold lining under the clouds. The mountain range west of their campsite was exceptionally high and that height brought early sunsets, but beautiful lights and mountain silhouettes. Laughter filled the air as the shepherds were feeling relaxed and safe. It was a good night for a party.

Clint had to occasionally interrupt the Mexican guards' fun as he sent out two at a time to patrol. These young guns loved the fun of a feast and the music, but like good soldiers, they took their turns on guard duty.

Early the next morning everyone was back to their tasks. The early stop the night before would mean no more stops before the ranch buildings would be reached. Clint let everyone know that the next campsite would be on the Rio Pecos Compound land. He informed the Basque herders that they would be coming up on his Navajo herders and their small herds of churro sheep. Since the Navajos, Basques, and Mexican guards all spoke Spanish, minimum trouble was anticipated. Clint would go ahead and alert the young Navajo girls that were tending their sheep up ahead. Keeping the herds separate would be a good idea. The white and plump bodies of the Merino-Churro cross looked a lot different than the much darker, long-haired, bare-bellied churros that the Navajos cherished. Also, both the Basque and the Navajos were owners of a share of their respective herds. It was going to require some cooperation from everyone if they were to keep ownership of the herds fair and straight.

Clint did not encounter any Navajo herders or sheep the next day. He decided to ride on into the night and finally reach his ranch house. The herds and the caravan would move at their usual steady pace. The Mexican guards had proven very reliable, even if young and obviously eager to get to Santa Fe.

Upon arriving at the compound, Clint went straight to the main Navajo Hogan. His arrival had been anticipated. One of the elder Navajo women was squatting beside a small mud oven, patiently waiting for his inquiry. A slow and rambling tale told Clint that the Navajo herd and its shepherds were well south and east of the ranch house. There had been some problems with coyotes on the western range, so they had had to move the sheep a day's ride east.

Clint could see a little concern on the wind-burned and usually stoic Indian face. The prospect of a large herd moving on to this grazing area would definitely compete with the small Indian herd. Outrage from the Navajo matriarch was not expected, but her only outward sign was a bit of raised eyebrow as she rambled on about the family, coyotes, and new lambs. She also hinted about another trip to Santa Fe to trade blankets. The permanent setup at the ranch house compound was proving very useful. Their largest loom had been repaired and reassembled in one of the sheds. The women were taking turns on this fine loom. Clint could see a bit of pride when the woman described her latest blanket designs. She was also reporting that the men had made some very good jewelry from the sliver and turquoise last traded. They would soon need a new supply of raw stones and silver. Clint knew that this rough-looking Navajo lady was the accepted leader of the clan. She was the owner of the most sheep and had the authority to negotiate for the group. Clint was tired and only wanted to find his bed in his own house, but there was something this spokeswoman wanted to address. Though it took a long and rambling path, the conversation finally got to the point.

The Navajos had a long-time goal of returning to their homeland in the giant red rock monument canyon. The large Apache land area north of their current location would make it almost impossible or at least very difficult to return to their homeland. The Navajo were familiar with the Basque people. They were very different and had not mixed well with the Navajos. The Basque men run everything. That is not the custom of the Navajos. This was the dilemma presented to Clint.

The arrival of the Basque herd two days later was handled without much controversy. The Navajo herd being held in the southeastern grazing area left the northern sections of the range open for the huge Basque herd. This Rio Pecos Compound range could handle two to three head per acre without over-grazing. Clint knew that his large ranch could handle 200,000 to 300,000 sheep annually. The challenge over the coming years was not grazing, but would be the marketing of 50,000 to 80,000 sheep per year.

Clint had to smile at himself for having this kind of problem. His saddlebags were full of gold, his ranch was well-stocked, and life was good. His long-term planning and conniving had paid off. The task now was to defend his holdings.

The Basque had selected an area on the north side of the ranch buildings for their permanent camp. This provided them good access to the well and ranch buildings. The Navajo hogans were on the southeast side of the Rio Pecos compound buildings. Both the Basque and Navajos enjoyed nomadic lifestyles, but being at the base camps really improved their day-to-day comforts.

It took only a couple of days for the Mexican guards to request their leave. These young men wanted to see the high life of Santa Fe. The slow, dusty sheep trail had worn out their patience. Girls, music and drinks were on their minds. Clint gave them a fatherly caution about the hazards of the big city. Then they were given a good bonus in gold coins and sent on their way. They left with a promise of work at the ranch if any of them wanted to return. Four of the older Mexican guards reluctantly agreed to wait a few weeks and accompany the Navajos on their Santa Fe trading trip. Surprisingly, some of the Basques also wanted to go. They had heard rumors that there were other Basque clans in or around Santa Fe and they also had a lot of trading to do for supplies.

Chapter 4

The four Mexican guards that were staying at the ranch were given the task of hunting down the coyotes. This gave them a chance to practice their rifle skills and put them in a place to scout the outer edges of the range. The Navajos requested the coyote skins for tanning. The thin, soft hides of the coyote were a useful item for trading, plus they could be made into clothing. After almost two weeks, the Mexican guards were ready to join their friends in Santa Fe. The Basque and Navajos had their hides, wool, blankets and jewelry packed and ready for travel with horses and wagons. The sale of any livestock would be made another time.

The trip to Santa Fe went without any problems. Clint had separated himself from the group so he could keep his secret identity separated from the people from the Rio Pecos compound. By riding some distance from the wagons, he could serve as the scout and no one in his trading party would even know that he was looking over them.

The Rio Pecos wagons pulled into the Santa Fe traders' camp near sunset and set up for the night. Clint snuck into his loft room in the stable without notice. The stabling of his horse made some noise, but Joe Black never came out of his quarters. A quick change of identity and Clint reemerged into the back alley as an unkempt hide-trading Mexican.

Information was his goal and saloons were the best source. It did not take long for Clint to spot his young Mexican guards, or at least three of them. He did not want to be recognized, so he kept his distance. The three young men were in one of the smaller and less flashy saloons. This surprised Clint. He had expected them to be partying with the best. Something was wrong.

Clint moved to another café and saloon for a quiet meal and more listening for gossip. He finally heard a reference to the four young Mexican gun hands. One of the guards had been drawn into a fight with a card player. The gambler had accused the young Mexican of cheating. The shooting was so quick that the young Mexican had never got his gun out of the holster. The local deputy sheriff ruled it a justified shooting. The gambler got off without a problem and took all the young dead man's money. When the other three friends tried to protest, the sheriff told them to either clear out of town or be quiet. The sheriff then claimed the downed guard's guns, gcar and horse for his office to cover expenses. The gossip told of similar tales about that saloon, that gambler and that specific deputy sheriff.

The horse the guard had been riding was one of Clint's better breeds. A little behind the scenes justice was in order. Clint had spent a good many nights with the downed guard and his friends around campfires on their long drive. Those young Mexican guards were as honest as anyone he knew. Clint was convinced the shooting had been deliberate and planned. Retribution would have to be carefully executed to avoid the three Mexican guards being suspected of a vengeful act.

Clint sent word back to the three guards about the traders' camp and where they could join up with their other friends. He was hoping the seven young men would sit tight and not charge back into town. Santa Fe seemed to be controlled by the Spanish families. Also powerful were the large money people from back east or from Europe. The Mexican people and the Indians were low men on the totem pole. The deputy sheriff that was protecting the gambler was probably paid by the saloon owners, the gambler or other interests. This kind of law was very common in the West. Clint would have to tread softly. A run out to the traders' camp tonight might head off a vengeful raid tomorrow.

A quick change of clothes and he was out at the traders' camp just in time. All seven guards had worked themselves into a rage, a demand to seek justice for their fallen companion.

Clint laid out the setup in Santa Fe. If they carried out direct revenge, it would be held against them. He asked that they allow him a few days to work something out. Their Basque and Navajo traders needed protection, plus he could use all of them as guards on the return trip to Rio Pecos. In spite of the anger that was close to the surface, these young guns were smart and could see the wisdom in Clint's advice. They agreed to avoid the Silver Spur Saloon while Clint worked out a safer scheme.

Clint found himself in a dilemma. He did not want to expose his true identify, but he also wanted to keep the rumor alive that anyone messing with Rio Pecos Compound people would be held accountable. The deterrence of that threat might save a lot of bloodshed. If he could convince the Mexican guards to escort the Basques and Navajos back to Rio Pecos, he would have time to deal with the gambler without getting the guards in trouble.

It only took two busy days on the market square for the Basques and Navajos to sell their wares. The ranch supplies were purchased the third morning and then they all headed back to Rio Pecos. The guards were not happy to leave unfinished business. But since the need to protect the families was a higher order of honor than revenge, they would wait to come back.

With all of the guards and Rio Pecos people out of town, Clint was able to go back undercover as a gambling hide-trader. The Silver Spur was his target and the breaking of the gambler was top priority. The gambler was a boastful type and a bluffer. Clint had observed him enough to know his every mood, stare and bluff. This gambler was not very good at countering the odds, thus, he depended on his deep pockets to buy most pots. This tactic would not work with Clint because of his wealth of gold, coins and dust.

It took some patience on Clint's part to get into the card game. A show of gold coins occasionally did finally trigger an invite to fill an empty seat. Clint could tell that the fancy, clean gambler with his ruffled shirt and fine jacket was not eager for the company of this roughly dressed Mexican. The prospects of new money were too great and his greed overrode his distaste for Clint's looks and accompanying odor.

Clint let the gambler buy a few pots before he made his move. The gambler's table stakes were transferred to Clint's side so smoothly that no one ever noticed. Clint had developed a habit of chewing mutton jerky. Every so often he would dig into his pockets to retrieve some. This misleading process allowed Clint to transfer coins from his table pile into his pocket. This kept his table stakes of chips and coins very modest. The other deception was to identify a player that was getting ready to leave the table. Clint could tell when a player was getting tired of the game. The trick was to let that player buy a couple of small pots, ensuring that they would leave with a small amount of money. This made it seem that winnings were being taken from the table by other players. This allowed Clint to continue draining the flashy gambler of his holdings.

A break in the game was called by the target gambler. It would resume in one hour. Clint knew that he had to get more money. This allowed Clint to unload some winnings, still keeping plenty to cover his action. During play, he had noticed a lot of eye contact passing between the gambler and the deputy sheriff. Both of them disappeared during the game break. Clint took the time to get a good meal and coffee, anticipating this last run may take some time.

The game resumed with the refreshed and dandified gambler buying drinks for the table. Clint knew this device well. Buy your opposition plenty of booze, fog his thinking and increase the other players' risk taking. Clint would pretend to drink heavily and get sloppy with his cards. He could read the gambler's plan to let Clint win a few small hands and make a big deal out of it. Then, the gambler would bluff everyone out of a big pot. This process went on for over two hours. Two of the other players ran out of money and were replaced by fresh players with money. Clint was keeping track so he did not lose ground during this tactic. In fact, he gradually increased his holdings by keeping most of it off the table. Clint could tell that the fancy gambler was so pleased with himself and his plan that he had not noticed Clint's steady winning.

Another break was requested, and again the gambler and the deputy sheriff left together and headed into a back room. Clint was sure the gambler was starting to realize how much he was losing, so this next series would be his last chance to clean out the gambler. The gambler and the lawman would have to be watched closely. Clint offered to switch seats with one of the fresh money players, saying it might change their luck. He could tell that this well-financed business man was not pleased with how the cards were running against him. The business man was very pleased with the offer to switch chairs. The new position gave Clint a better view of the deputy sheriff and the rear door. The mirrors that Clint could now see provided him a complete view of the saloon.

The third round of gambling started with the fancy gambler buying more drinks, including a bottle for the table. From what Clint read in the faces of the gambler and the lawman, this was going to be the big kill. The series of play was well into the eighth hand when the fancy gambler tried to buy a large pot. He had made two bold raises to build up the kitty, then a giant raise to bluff three of the six players out. The fourth round was another monster raise that took the fourth player out, leaving only Clint and the gambler face-to-face over a huge pile of chips and gold coins.

The gambler then raised more than Clint had on the table. The gambler reached out to drag in the stack of money. Clint slowly pulled a leather pouch out of his pocket and tossed it on the table. "If you can match that, it's a call. If not, the stakes are mine," he said. In amazement, the businessman leaned over and poured the pouch out onto the table. He counted out almost $1,000-worth of $20 gold pieces.

The gambler was caught in his own trap. He did not have enough cash with him to call. The other players were quick to remind the gambler of the house rules. You could not leave the table to acquire more funds.

The next action had been anticipated by Clint. The lawman had moved around to a position directly behind him. The fancy gambler then accused Clint of cheating. Through a mirror, Clint could see the deputy pulling his gun at the same time the gambler was clearing the table with his pistol. Clint rolled over his chair and kicked the table against the gambler. The roar of gunfire filled the saloon. When the smoke cleared, both the gambler and the lawman were dead. Clint slipped his gun back into its holster after replacing three shells. He then crawled out from under the table and declared that they had shot each other. This idea planted that scene into everyone's mind so that the whole audience told that same story to the marshal when he arrived to investigate. Two other people had been hit with flying lead, but they were not life-threatening injuries. Clint had gathered his winnings during all the excitement, before the marshal got there.

Clint was told how lucky he was because that gambler had killed six men over the last couple of years. In fact, he had killed a young, good-looking Mexican man only a few days earlier. His habit was to accuse one of the players of cheating and shoot him. The lawman was always a witness and would then declare the gunfight justified. The businessman again impressed on Clint how lucky he was to have survived the gunfight. If they had not shot each other, they would have shot him cold even though he was hiding under the table.

The doctor had arrived and he declared both men dead. The gambler's ruffled shirt had been removed for the doctor's examination. It was this shirt that Clint sneaked out of the saloon along with all his loot. There was so much turmoil that no one even suspected that Clint had shot both men. The marshal had taken his investigation serious enough to examine all the players' guns. The only expended shells were in the lawman's and gambler's guns. The four players were released.

When they heard the complete story, the seven Mexican guards felt that justice had indeed been served. The blood-stained, ruffled shirt, a handful of gold coins, and the slain guard's horse were all returned to Rio Pecos Compound.

Chapter 5

The gun battle at the Silver Spur Saloon that had left two men dead also brought way too much attention to Clint, even though he kept repeating an image of himself as hiding under the table. The death of a lawman focused more attention than was usual for a gambling dispute. It did help that no one had liked the fancy, arrogant gambler and besides the deputy sheriff had been involved too many times with this gambler in previous shootings. It was time to get out of Santa Fe for a while.

Clint was awakened that night by some loud talking coming from below him in the stable. It was Joe Black's voice, but the other commanding voice was new to Clint. Although the exchange of words could not be fully understood, Joe Black was being chewed-out and threatened with eviction. This surprised Clint, who had always assumed that Joe was the owner.

The next day was a low-profile one for Clint, who needed to deposit his surplus monies in the bank. He knew it was not safe to carry around gold coins. He needed to contact Mr. Jenson at the bank, but he was known to Jenson as the honorable Cliff Martinez, a rancher and major property holder down on the Rio Pecos. In the past, Mr. Jenson had assisted Cliff Martinez with a banker down south in Crossbow in Manatee County by the name of Brad Mason.

Clint had to be very careful or the clean-up and change of clothes might not fool some of the people in Santa Fe. After the shooting, the close contact with so many people could be a real problem. If he could put some time between that incident and his reappearance, his risk would be reduced. But the need to put all that gold into the bank was pressing Clint to take the chance of being recognized.

His first act was to clean-up and slip out of the stable bunk room. If he could get past Joe Black and down the alley into the foot traffic on the street, then the walk to the bank would not be too tough.

However, once inside the bank, if any of the customers or clerks had been at the Silver Spur Saloon yesterday, the deception may fail. Finally, Clint decided to take his chance, and his fairly expensive clothing, neat appearance and very businesslike approach seemed to work. He was escorted into Mr. Jenson's office after a very short wait. Mr. Jenson only knew Clint as Cliff Martinez, a large depositor with his bank, so the hope was that the presentation of another large deposit of gold coins would make more of an impression on the banker than the sloppy hide-trader who delivered it.

Clint happened to view himself in a mirror as he was turning to leave Jenson's office. He hardly recognized himself, so his worries may have been exaggerated. Still, a fast retreat was called for. The cleaning of the stable loft room took a little more time, but he didn't want to leave behind any trace of Cliff Martinez. Future visits to the Santa Fe bank would have to be staged from another safe place. If Joe Black's stable was searched, all they would find is a bunk suitable for simple Mexican hide-trader.

Clint was making a wide circle around the market traders' camping area when he spotted the settlers that they had helped on the trail up toward Raton Pass. From a distance, it looked as though those settlers had just flopped here in complete despair. It had been several months since Clint had helped these people on their trip from Kansas to Santa Fe. They were in trouble again and he felt compelled to inquire as to their condition.

The settlers were very leery when he approached their camp. Clint called out when he was close enough to be heard, but far enough back to not get shot. He explained that it was his group of sheep herders that had helped them up north. He was allowed to enter the camp, and from there, it didn't take long for their tale of woe to spill out.

They had finally arrived in Santa Fe expecting a city with normal eastern services, law, order and peace. What they found was a ruthless, free-for-all, corrupt town. Gambling and music halls were open night and day, seven days a week. The two large Spanish churches did not take well to the settlers' Protestant religion. Women were being harassed on the streets and their young men lured into the dance halls and gambling houses. Their few possessions had been looted and two of their group had even been killed by random gunfire.

They could not stay in this place, but they had no money to return east. Every member of the group of men, women and children was scared to death and hopeless. Clint knew the first thing to do was provide a good meal for everyone. Quickly, he scoured the other camps and bought meat, flour and all the fresh ingredients he could find. The settlers were put to work making bread, roasting the side of beef and preparing some space for a feast. The directed activity raised their spirits immediately. The busy work took their minds off their dire situation. Clint had purchased some sugar from one of the camps, and one lady got busy making treats for the kids.

The hungry children were fed first. This put life back into them and off they took running and playing like normal kids. Fresh coffee was enjoyed after the big meal with a lot of appreciation showered onto Clint. Finally, the conversation came back to their plight. It took some probing questions for Clint to find out what they had originally planned on doing for a living. The group consisted of several builders, carpenters, brick masons, farmers and a school teacher. They had planned on building themselves houses and a church when they found a place to settle. They had been told back east that each family could homestead 160 acres. This size of farm back east would have been huge, but out here they could not raise enough on 160 acres to sustain one family. To these eastern settlers, this land around Santa Fe looked worthless.

Clint presented a temporary solution for the entire group. The Rio Pecos Compound was expanding. A new, very large herd of sheep had just arrived along with shepherds' families. Buildings were needed, children needed schooling, and gardens needed to be developed down by the river. The compound was fairly safe, but everyone needed to learn to shoot and participate in guarding the ranch. If they wanted to join the Rio Pecos Compound, there would be new skills to learn. The primary products being produced by the ranch were wool, hides, mutton, blankets and jewelry. If they would join the compound for a year, it would give them enough time to earn the money to return east. If they learned to adapt to the West and wanted to stay, Rio Pecos Compound might develop into a good place for them.

There wasn't much to discuss among themselves because other options were not available. A relaxed calm fell over the camp that night as the glimmer of hope started to appear in these settlers.

The difficulty would be the transport of these settlers back out the Santa Fe Trail to Rio Pecos. Much of their stock had been hurt or stolen. Their wagons were not in good shape and their food supply was exhausted.

Clint decided to go back to the stable manager Joe Black for assistance. Wagons needed repairs, more horses and also a couple of guards to escort the settlers to Rio Pecos were needed. It was late that night when Clint made his way back to his loft room. While he had decided not to disturb Joe tonight, Joe came out of his quarters as Clint was putting his horse away. The request was simple and straightforward. Clint wanted to hire Joe to repair the settlers' wagons and rent a few horses to pull these wagons up the Santa Fe Trail to the Rio Pecos Compound. If two guards could be found, it would help a lot. The guards could then bring the rental horses back to Joe. Joe was glad to help. He needed the work and he knew two young men that would make the trip out and bring back the spare horses for a few dollars.

Clint finally got a restless night's sleep in the loft. The sun was just coming up over the mountain peaks as he pulled into the settlers' camp. A fire was going and hot coffee was ready. Joe Black and two helpers would be out before noon. The settlers were to have the wagon problems identified so Joe could get to work on them immediately. The two helpers would assist them in their travels and bring back the rental horses. Clint would ride on ahead and have some of the ranch guards bring more horses out to meet them on the trail.

After only one night on the trail, Clint was back at the ranch. The recognition of the gambler's ruffled shirt, complete with bullet holes and blood finally put to rest urge for revenge that all seven young guns had brewing deep within their hearts. Besides, the mercy trip out to gather the settlers put the young men in a good frame of mind. They would leave immediately with extra pull horses and a few supplies.

His house was neat and clean, with a pot of coffee on the wood stove. It sure was good to be home. Although he had spent very little time in his ranch house, it did feel like all the comforts of home: a place to put his things, a nice clean bed, and a feeling of security and peace. His vision for a small village to grow up in this valley was starting to materialize.

Chapter 6

The arrival of the settlers in Rio Pecos Compound caused quite a stir. The Navajos expressed some concern that they might get pushed out. The Basque wanted to keep their nomadic way of life. Setting up a permanent village with houses was not their way. However, they would appreciate a trading post or supply store being available to them. The new settlers from the east wanted to build wood houses and a church. These settlers only knew wood frame construction with wood floors. Their first impression of the adobe buildings was not positive.

The settlers were assigned an area near the ranch house and within walking distance to the community well. Each group would be self-sufficient and separate. Clint's idea of community may have to wait awhile.

The settlers set up a tent city using both wagons and extra tents. If they decided to stay through the winter, then shelters would have to be built. Logs and lumber were in short supply down in this valley. Lumber-size trees only grew much higher in the mountains where the rain fall was sufficient. The available building material was clay for adobe bricks and there were two excellent clay pits near the compound. Retraining the eastern carpenters and masons to use adobe was proving to be a challenge.

The Basque had proven to be good shepherds. The lamb crop was large. They would need to sell a large number of sheep within the year. The nearby range had proven to be in great shape for raising sheep. The Basque were reporting that this valley was even better than the high plains of Texas. There was a lot more shelter from the wind and the vegetation variety seemed to be better for the sheep. The Basque were fairly content with the set up as long as the eastern settlers didn't try to build fences or push their religion. Besides, the New Mexico Territory had a climate very similar to their ancestral homes in the mountains of Spain.

The Mexican guards had done a good job of controlling the pesky coyote population. Also, there had only been two instances where riders had entered the valley off the Santa Fe Trail. Those riders were greeted with a show of force sufficient to prevent violence. The guards were pretty sure the two separate groups of riders were not connected, but both parties behaved like rustlers or thieves. So far the ranch had not lost any livestock nor had anyone been hurt for months.

The Mexican guards were given the chore of breaking the horses in addition to escort and guard duties, as well as training everyone to shoot and defend themselves.

The school teacher was set-up with a classroom in the ranch house dining room. The teacher had agreed that religion would be left to the families. She would teach reading, writing and math. One person from both the Navajo and Basque families would also teach a trade of blanket weaving, jewelry making, and sewing. This cooperation and joint participation succeeded in getting all the children into the school. It was Clint's hope the children would gradually bring tolerance of diversity to the adults. The other major objective was to produce the skills necessary for the development and growth of the compound.

Clint was very surprised at the number of books these settlers had lugged across the mountains. They had given up most of their possessions for the trip west. While the major portion of what they had brought had been looted or destroyed, it turned out that the western bandits were not interested in books, and these eastern settlers set a high priority on education for their children. This would prove very beneficial for all the families at Rio Pecos Compound.

Although everything was working fairly smoothly for this odd collection of people, Clint could see the development of stress cracks. The Navajos would like to return to their ancestral homes. Three or four of the Mexican guards would like to move to Santa Fe or even return to Mexico City. They were starting to think of families of their own. Meanwhile, the Basque seemed very content, but the need for a major sheep herd drive was building. It was getting to be time to cull the herd and make some money.

The eastern settlers were in constant discussion about their choices to either stay, return east or travel on westward. Several families had settled in very well and seemed quite content. One of the major religious leaders of the group wanted to move into Santa Fe and start a church. He felt that the real need for Christian work was in that sin city called Santa Fe. The decision to keep religious teachings out of the compound school had not been acceptable to him. He was constantly pushing his point of view every chance that came along. The families with children were always reminding him and others of the ruthless nature of the big city. The school teacher and several of the mothers were very pleased with how things were working for them and their families at the compound.

The whole community had worked together to build a large, long adobe building that had several rooms. Two rooms were set aside for the school; others rooms were for weaving and for wool storage. All connected to a big supply store and trading post. An agreement was reached by three people to run the supply store and trading post. Clint had not been involved, but to his surprise, one settler, one Navajo and one Basque had worked out this arrangement and presented it to him. If Clint would underwrite the initial set-up cost, then the ownership would be split equally between the four partners. Everyone seemed very pleascd with this opportunity.

The initial store was set up by crediting each contributor for their contribution. The first couple of weeks were more like a trading session where people brought in their surplus items and took out things they were short of. The three store owners soon had their first major supply list. A caravan would take to market wool, blankets, jewelry and mutton with five guards. They would carry a bank draft so that Mr. Jenson at the Santa Fe bank could issue extra money to cover the purchases. If the trading went in their favor, very little extra funding would be needed.

Most of the women and children would stay at the compound even though trouble was not expected. This would be an extensive trading session plus lots of heavy loading and unloading. Clint would not be a part of this caravan. These new merchants would be on their own to purchase, bargain, and trade for their store and community. Two of the Mexican guards would not return with the wagons if they could find employment in Santa Fe. Clint knew he would need to provide some back-up patrol work for the loaded supply wagon during their return trip.

It took two full days for the wagons to be loaded before leaving the ranch and the in-bound trip to Santa Fe went without any problems. It took all week to sell and trade the materials, then two more days to purchase the items on the very large shopping list.

The two young Mexican guards that wanted to stay in Santa Fe did find some work with one of the large landholders just north of Santa Fe, near Española. Clint had taken back his disguise as hide-trader, kept his distance and stayed out of sight. His people were not aware of his protective oversight. The loaded wagons headed back to Rio Pecos would be the inviting target. Those onlookers with thievery on their minds were easily attracted by the large amount of purchases and the heavily loaded wagons.

Clint could see from his lookout that his people were spending another night at the traders' campsite after they were loaded. This delay would give any troublemakers a chance to organize and get out in front to set an ambush. It was good that Clint's powerful spyglass did give him good coverage of the trails out of Santa Fe.

While he watched there had been some traffic on the main trail out of Santa Fe toward Gloriata Pass, but only one group of six riders concerned Clint. He had spotted two of these men spying on the Rio Pecos wagons. The two joined the other four riders and moved on eastward up the main Santa Fe Trail. Their suspicious behavior was enough to lead Clint to follow them. Sure enough, very soon, all six riders took positions on both sides of the trail where it passed through a narrow gorge. The rock outcrops on each side would serve as excellent vantage points from which to ambush the wagon train. Clint's estimate put his wagons arriving at the ambush point at about noon the next day.

The next morning, the six would-be bushwhackers watched as a lonely Mexican hide-trader passed through the gorge below them pulling one pack horse. From their high post, they could make out the dust trail of the wagon train in the distance about an hour's time or more away. Gradually the hide-trader disappeared around the next bend and was gone.

The six outlaws moved down closer to the trail, setting up a deadly crossfire with three guns on each side of the trail. This would be like shooting rabbits in a cage. The first two wagons were just coming into the narrow passageway when one of the bandits jerked and fell over the rocks into the trail dust below. The crack of the rifle followed a split-second later.

Then a second shot rang out and another bushwhacker screamed out. This time the sound came from the other direction. The bandits realized they had been spotted and out flanked. A mad dash out the trail away from the wagons was their only hope. Two of the four remaining would-be robbers made the dash. The two escaping riders had left four of their comrades laying in the dust paying with their lives for an attempted ambush.

When the wagon train pulled safely through the gorge, two saddle horses were tied beside the trail with spare guns hooked to the saddle horns. The Mexican guards rounded up the other two horses and their owners' guns. The final leg of the trip to Rio Pecos was made in peace and quiet. Wagons and guards were met by Clint and by all the waiting families at their new store.

The tales around the campfire and over dinner tables that night included one about a note on the trail that told of an upcoming ambush. The story was expanded to include a mystery shooter or guardian angel. As usual, the story got bigger with each telling.

Chapter 7

The small Rio Pecos village gradually settled into a comfortable routine, and the trading post became the common meeting place. It provided a place to work out the rough edges between the various groups. Sometimes it even served more like a court where grievances were aired, disputes were settled and community rules explained or amended. One of the benefits of this neutral meeting place was the presentation of both sides of an issue to silence wild rumors.

One of the rumors brought back by the supply train concerned a sheep drive from Española north to the Colorado mines. One of the big sheep ranches north of Santa Fe, the Bond Ranch, was organizing the drive. People could join the drive with their own herders or they could sell their sheep at a discount. The Bond Ranch was offering three cents per head now. The current estimated price up near Durango was five to seven cents per head. It appeared that the Bond Ranch drive was an annual event.

The community decision was to sell this first cull herd at Española for the three cents. Next year the Navajos would help herd their share of sheep to Durango. This would put them close to their native land. After considerable additional discussion, it was decided that two Mexican guards and two Navajos would make the trip to Durango to sell the herd.

The two young Mexican guards were hoping for some adventure. Durango might be just the place with its gold and silver mines and lots of hustle and bustle. The two Navajos would be scouting out the area for their own people and a possible new future. A new supply of silver would be very helpful if it could be purchased reasonably at the mines. If all four of them decided to stay, a message would be sent back with the Bond Ranch herders.

The two Mexican guards were then sent to the Bond Ranch to confirm the sheep drive and the conditions for adding the Rio Pecos sheep. In the meantime, the Rio Pecos Compound herds would be culled. If the Bond Ranch drive did not work out, then an independent drive to Santa Fe or even Tucumcari would be undertaken.

The Rio Pecos cull herd was pulled together by the time word came back from Española. The Bond Ranch said they would appreciate the additional sheep. Sr. Bond would pay four cents per head with the assistance of the four men on the Durango drive. The Rio Pecos addition to the drive would be about 10,000 sheep and four men. Clint organized a herding party of twelve to deliver the sheep to the Bond Ranch. The trail to Española was fairly easy going. The sheep herd would be taken through the Gloriata Pass and down into the Rio Grande valley, then upstream to Española. These trails had been used by the Spaniards for over 200 years. These old herding routes went from the Gulf of Mexico up the Rio Grande through Santa Fe and Española, then split at the Rio Chama for two different routes north to the mining towns and the east-west trails.

The meeting with Josa Bond, the large Spanish grant holder near Española, went smoothly. He was a gracious and lavish host. His family had been one of the first Spanish families to establish sheep ranching in the upper Rio Grande valley. His great grandfather had helped the Spanish Army occupy Santa Fe capital. The Spanish government rewarded his family with a huge grant of land that had been claimed by the Pueblo Indians. Thus, Sr. Bond maintained a sizeable army to protect his land grant and to keep peace with the Indians. The more accurate term for the Indian's arrangement was confinement to designated Indian reservations. The Mexican government had also paid Josa to maintain control in this area until the New Mexico Territory was eventually taken over by the U.S. Government. While the current rule of law was in flux, Sr. Bond explained that he was the law on his land grant.

As per their agreement, Josa Bond turned over the gold payment when the Rio Pecos herd count was completed. He had to tell Clint that he would probably get seven to eight cents per head at the gold and silver mines up north. He was a very proud man and liked to brag about his good fortune.

He put on a big feast that night before the herd would head north. There were six other ranches that also had contributed to the drive. During dinner Clint was given a place of honor among the other ranch owners at the head table. Both music and the food were the best that Clint could remember.

During the evening celebration, he did pick up some very useful information. Sr. Bond owned a sawmill just northeast of Santa Fe, up near the large pine tree line. He cut lumber commercially for the Santa Fe building market. The sawmill had all the wagons and teamsters needed to deliver the lumber. Clint arranged for four loads of choice lumber to be delivered to the Rio Pecos Compound.

Clint would carry the order from Sr. Bond to the sawmill on his way back to Rio Pecos. This would give Clint a chance to inspect the quality of the lumber and give them specific instructions on type and size needed.

The team of men that had delivered the sheep to Sr. Bond decided to escort the lumber wagons back to Rio Pecos, knowing there would be more safety in numbers. Everyone was eager to get the much-needed lumber back home. The construction of shelters and other buildings had been held up due to the lack of lumber.

The settlers' skills working with adobe brick had not noticeably improved. These wood carpenters would be very pleased to receive sawmill lumber to work with. The settlers needed additional shelter before winter set in. They had already spent one winter in their wagons and tents and this winter they were looking forward to the comfort of real homes.

The Navajos had built themselves large permanent mud and stick hogans near the ranch house and well. In addition, they had put up several modest hogans out in the range making this as good as it had ever been. However, a split was developing in the group. The older leaders wanted to move back to their ancestral groups up north. Some of the middle-aged families that remembered the hardships they had endured up north wanted to stay on Rio Pecos Compound. The young teenage bucks hearing all the old stories from the elders also wanted to go north to the giant stone monument valley. It was these young men that were anxiously waiting for a report of the sheep drive to Durango.

The Basque shepherds were the only completely settled group. They had recreated their lifestyle of old. The only change was the adoption of Navajo hogan construction methods. The Basque built large permanent family hogans at the ranch base camp. In addition, they had copied the Navajo pattern of building semi-permanent shelters on the high elevations for summer grazing and on the warmer valley area for winter grazing.

The seasonal movement of the herds from valley to the mountain and back again was a lot more efficient with these camps. They did not have to haul so much building materials for shelters.

The Navajo-style structures used local materials of sticks and mud and were very durable with an annual maintenance of mud plaster. These building designs also saved a lot of sheep hides that could then be sold rather than being used for tent shelters. The arrival of the lumber wagons set off a frenzy of construction. The Kansas settlers were the most energized. Their skills with wood were finally put to use. The houses materialized rapidly with all the same design, wood shake roofs and rough board floors.

The lead preacher of the settlers did not push very much for a church buildings, since he was still promoting the move to Santa Fe where a mission church could be built. While he had several followers, the majority of settlers wanted to build their new houses and stay at the Rio Pecos Compound. A community was starting to develop in spite of the vast differences in culture, work methods, and goals. The work of building enabled most of the families to be well housed by the time the first major cold wave hit.

All four of the men that had gone with the Bond Ranch sheep drive to Durango returned just as the bad weather rolled in. Their report and their stories were shared around the large stove at the trading post.

The two young Mexican guards had really enjoyed the Durango visit, but the safer surroundings of Rio Pecos had brought them back. The two Navajos had contacted a couple of Navajo families in the Durango sheep yards. Then the Navajos had brought their blankets, wool and mutton to the miners for sale and to trade for silver and turquoise stones. They reported abundant grasslands and opens spaces ready to be used, although there were still some problems with the Hopi and Apache Indians. While the miners were moving across the area, they stayed mostly in the steep parts of the mountains. Settlers from the east usually passed on through the lower semi-arid lands headed to California. Trade with wagon trains and miners was very profitable.

The Navajos had also brought back a couple of bags of silver and stones. The prices in Durango were cheaper than Santa Fe. However, the sale price of the finished jewelry was also a lot lower in Durango as compared to the market square in Santa Fe.

Clint settled up with all the families and the sheep owners according to their contribution to the drive. The Mexican guards were also given a bonus for their work in addition to their regular salaries. This had been a very profitable year and the future was looking even better. The families could head into winter with warm homes and gold coins in their pockets.

Chapter 8

Spring came with a sudden burst of flowers, new green growth and noisy children playing outside. The new lamb crop was even better than expected. The push would be on come fall for another major drive to get the sheep to market.

While Clint did not want to over-graze his range, he also wanted to constantly improve his herd. Culling out the worst of the sheep each year would gradually lead to a superior herd.

The winter's weaving had produced some beautiful blankets. Even though the Basque and the Navajos did not socialize, the woven designs were beginning to combine the best of both. The much finer wool of the Basque sheep was finding its way into the course weaving patterns of Navajo blankets. Natural dyes that each culture had developed over the years were varied. As they shared these dye secrets, colors were produced that had not been seen before in the markets around the Santa Fe square. The Rio Pecos blankets as they were beginning to be known drew top-dollar bids.

After the winter, the trading post and storage rooms became rather bare. The finished products of blankets and jewelry were starting to accumulate. A major trading trip to Santa Fe was needed as soon as the weather and roads permitted.

The lead preacher had convinced two of the settler families to join him in his move to Santa Fe. The money they had made building homes for the other settlers and the buildings for Clint's ranch would see them through for a few months. Both families were pretty good carpenters, and besides, the preacher was a good helper when he put his mind to it. Santa Fe had a lot of building going on as more people arrived every year. The lumber drivers of the Bond Ranch had given the preacher the names of several landowners in Santa Fe. So along with the preacher, two families would make the trip with the supply train. As well as possible, the settlers' wagons had been repaired over the winter. Even though the village did not have a blacksmith, Clint had set up a shop with forge and the needed supplies. Everyone did their best to repair wagons, saddles and harnesses, and to shoe the horses.

This trading trip would be a major event. Most of the people would go this time. A few of the Basque and Navajo herders would stay to tend the herds. One of the settler families would also stay at the ranch and look after things. Two of the Mexican guards would stay with the ranch. About 200 sheep were to be driven along with the supply train. These sheep would then be dressed out and sold as mutton when they arrived at the traders' campsite just outside of Santa Fe. The first two days went slowly. The sheep traveled at a rate of less than fifteen miles per day. After two days of this, it was decided that the wagon train would go ahead to set up camp and open their booths at the market square. The herd would arrive several days later, and then the mutton would be put on sale.

The trip agreement was the same as last time. Each group would handle its own trading and the purchase of its own supplies. Clint would not be a part of the caravan. The Mexican guards would provide protection. If additional funds were needed to restock the trading post, a bank withdrawal could be arranged with Mr. Jenson. The ranch's share of the sales should be more than enough to restock the Rio Pecos store and trading post. Two of the three store managers were making the trip and they would handle the money and the re-supply.

Clint took two extra horses and went directly to Santa Fe. This put him several days ahead of the supply train. His stable loft room was as he had left it. Joe Black was working hard at cleaning up the stalls when Clint arrived. A brief conversation covered weather, new people in town and payment for his room for another year. Joe let Clint know that the landlord was changing things, thus Joe could not guarantee that Clint's room would always be available. Clint read some worry and concern in Joe's face and voice.

Clint reassured him that the room had been a great help and if it wasn't available sometime in the future that would be okay. Clint appreciated the support that Joe had already given him. This spare-room deal had been a win-win for them both.

This trip into Santa Fe was a test run to see if the past saloon shootout at the Silver Spur would cause him any problems. After a few hands of cards at the Silver Spur, he was soon relieved of his worries. The only mention of the incident was a slur about him hiding under the tables. These western men put a high value on bravery and toughness. This Mexican hide-trader was low on their list even before that show of cowardice. He had become almost an invisible man in the crowd . . . just as he wanted. The next stop was the Golden Mint where Clint had been told the questionable owner of Joe's stable hung out. It did not take long for Clint to spot his next target. Claude Johnson was an overweight, over-dressed, pushy gent. Clint noticed at least two gunmen that seemed to be watching over him. The back table gambling group was out of Clint's dress code. The thing to do now was to observe and learn as much as possible about this man and his method of operation. Three days of circulating in and out of the Golden Mint and other cafés and saloons built up a picture of this man in Clint's mind.

Claude Johnson had arrived in Santa Fe five or six years earlier with obvious money. He had purchased a good size ranch outside of town and also a couple of small businesses in town. He always had two or three guards near him. A few shop owners hinted that Mr. Johnson may have used his guards as muscle forcing a below-market sales price for the businesses he purchased. In addition, at least two different people expressed the opinion that Claude Johnson had taken ownership of Joe Black's stable. The Mexican Army had left in a hurry leaving Joe Black behind, so these local shop owners thought that by rights of occupancy, Joe should own the stable and blacksmith equipment. The rumor had it that Mr. Johnson had presented a paper to the land office giving him title, but this paper didn't show up until several years after Mr. Johnson had moved into the area.

A visit to the land office provided Clint a big jolt. Posted on the inside wall were several notices of land disputes. One of those notices identified title to the Rio Pecos land being challenged by Claude Johnson. A survey by one of the railroad companies was cited as the source for challenging the title held by Brad Mason and Cliff Martinez.

The land title challenge had only been submitted within the past two weeks. A 60-day public posting of the dispute was required before a hearing could be held. The challenging party would then make its case before the land office staff. If there was merit in the challenge, then a public hearing would be held before the territory judge. The old Spanish land grants were being challenged frequently. The courts seemed to be supporting the eastern settlers rather than the old Spanish families. The original huge land grant holdings were gradually being torn apart or at least reduced in size.

Clint knew that his land had been surveyed and recorded. If a new survey was being used to challenge the boundaries, that new survey was probably a fraud. It would take some time to track down and uncover this shady deal. Besides, it was going to be extra tough because his brother Brad knew nothing of this entire land deal and then complicating matters even more was Clint's double identity.

The signatures on both Joe Black's stable title work and Rio Pecos land were the same. Claude Johnson was the proposed owner of both with the same three witnesses. Clint copied down the names of the witnesses, and the surveyor.

The surveyor's name had a familiar ring. He had been on another survey crew when Clint was doing survey work. Most of the survey group was crooked and greedy. In fact, it was that surveyor's greed that had given Clint the chance to acquire his vast track of land. Solving this problem was going to be tricky. If his true identity was discovered through the tie to his brother Brad, he could be jailed on the old arrest warrant.

Clint's appearance had changed so much from a small, wiry 16-year-old with a hot temper to a mature, solidly-built and tall body. It was unlikely that his young enemies would recognize him by sight. However, a link by name or association would be more likely.

It was the fifth day before Clint spotted some of the Rio Pecos people at the market square. He kept his distance, but was on the lookout for any problems. It looked like his people were doing a brisk business. In fact they might complete their trading before the sheep even arrived. The whole group was having a great time without knowing that the ranch they were depending on was under a challenge for ownership. If Clint could have it work his way, that problem would be solved before it ever confronted them.

The banker, Mr. Jenson, would have to be contacted to see if Claude Johnson had made any claims against his ranch. This meant that changing back into his business suit would increase the risk of being identified. He had moved all his clothes out of the stable loft room the last time he stayed. Joe Black did not seem to pay any attention to his comings and goings. It appeared that Joe was having problems of his own. So, Clint moved his stuff back into the stable loft.

The meeting with Mr. Jenson went well. No claim had yet been made against the ranch. This suggested to Clint that Johnson was trying to slip his new survey through without anyone noticing. If the hearings could be held without dispute, very likely the land title office would accept the new survey and transfer title.

Clint made another handsome bank deposit. His behind the scenes gathering of information from saloon to saloon was very profitable. His skill at cards, the lack of any good competition and lots of available cash made for big winnings and little notice. Each table take was small and he moved often.

Twice he spotted some of his Mexican guards, but wasn't recognized by them. The young guards were much too interested in the young ladies to focus on a common hide-trader.

His daily inspection of the campsite finally paid off. The sheep herd arrived at last, and the slaughter and meat processing were all completed.

Clint stepped up his surveillance because the money and supplies were mounting. This often brought out the crooks. He was pleased with the improvement in his young guards. They had increased their presence and alertness. The young men were an impressive sight, with their black saddles trimmed with silver, fancy guns and excellent horses. They had broken and trained some of Clint's best stock and took pride in showing them off. Hopefully, this show of force would be enough to ward off the usual lazy bandit.

It may also serve the Rio Pecos traders well that word was spreading about anyone who messed with these people often disappearing or dying. A mysterious protector seemed to be looking over the people from Rio Pecos.

When Clint was satisfied that his people were as well protected as possible in the lawless territory, he got back to addressing the legal challenge to his land ownership. The most direct way would be to assassinate Claude Johnson. While this had a certain appeal to Clint, it also pricked a little of his ruthless nature.

Although Mr. Johnson had made a lot of enemies with his unethical dealings and his overly flamboyant manner, it might bring suspicions back to Rio Pecos as a clear beneficiary of his death. Clint called forth a little more patience and deliberation out of his soul. If Claude Johnson had heard the rumors about the protection afforded the Rio Pecos Compound, then maybe a stern warning would get him to back off. Sending a note to Johnson stating the facts of the true survey and a warning of dire consequences was a good idea. This warning, if ignored, would clear Clint's conscience if he had to take more drastic measures.

If Clint could get the message to Johnson while the Rio Pecos young guns were still in town, it might have more effect. The problem of this idea was that his Mexican guards would not be aware of the pressure their presence might put on Claude Johnson. This could place his guards at greater risk if Johnson was not bluffed. Clint would need to be present when Johnson opened the note so he could read his face and reaction.

Clint's superior skill in reading people would be very critical. If Johnson decided to take action, he might have his many guards take out the young Mexican protectors.

Clint prepared the note and made his way to the Golden Mint Saloon. Claude Johnson sat at his favorite table where the dealer always provided him the same seat. This group was made-up of ranch owners, businessmen and well-dressed gamblers. It was not a table that a poorly-dressed working-class Mexican could join. However, if Clint wanted to watch the body language and facial expressions, Claude needed to receive his note during the card game. Clint watched the game for over an hour before an idea presented itself. Claude Johnson always had a barmaid bring him a shot of rye whiskey after every hour of play. His special bottle was brought on a tray and the shot was poured in front of him. It was somewhat a show of style and very much an arrogant display of wealth and power. You could tell that Johnson was a little sweet on the very pretty young barmaid, who was the only one that served him.

The trick was to get the note onto that tray in a way that Johnson would notice it. It had to pass the barmaid's inspection until the drink was served. Clint had noticed that the bartender used little folded cards to send out bar bills to special guests. A quick slip-of-hand by Clint secured one of the cards to the tray with the note inside.

As the waitress moved through the saloon headed to the rear table, a slight bump and the card was on the tray without anyone noticing. Then, Clint casually moved to a good vantage point. The process worked beautifully. Johnson opened the card and took out the note. As he read it, a look of alarm and fright showed ever so slightly across his poker face. He played one more hand, and then excused himself. This was followed by a brief conversation with the barmaid. Her protests of innocence were apparent even from Clint's distance. The following discussion with the bartender was much longer, and it led to a scan of the saloon searching for a guilty face. Clint was passed over without much attention. Soon, Johnson's guards joined him and they left the saloon.

The bartender was giving the barmaid the third degree when Clint slipped out the side door of the saloon. He suspected that Johnson had posted watchmen outside to identify anyone leaving in a hurry or acting suspiciously. Clint moved into the shadows and waited. His eyes adjusted to the dark, then he slowly moved to inspect his escape route. The guard on the back alley was not very attentive. He was smoking, so a cigarette glow was visible, plus Clint could smell the smoke. The lookout was restless and moving around a lot. This made it easy for Clint to sneak up on him and lay the butt of his gun upside his head. Johnson's man dropped like a rock. The sound did not bring anyone, so Clint stripped the man of his belt and gun, then slipped on down the alley to the stable.

After stowing the downed guard's gun and gear, he then moved up to Main Street to monitor the movement of Johnson and his men. There must have been six or seven heavily armed men moving up and down Main Street looking for trouble. Clint had hoped that the note would cause Johnson to pull back and be more cautious. It may have had the opposite effect. Clint did notice that no law officers were in on the search, so apparently Johnson had not reported the threat to the sheriff's office.

It wasn't long before two gun hands came to the stable and rousted out Joe Black. They wanted to know if anyone had taken their horses out in the past hour. The men were rather rough on Joe as they looked throughout the stable. One of them climbed into the loft and busted into Clint's room. He slapped Clint around a little, mostly out of frustration. Clint took the roughing-up like a coward and the gunman left.

When Clint climbed down out of the loft, Joe was apologizing to him for the trouble. Joe and Clint had a little laugh between them over the poor job the gunmen had done on them. They joked that they had been hit harder by angry women than these lightweight troublemakers.

After a few hours, Johnson and eight riders pulled out of town. Clint could tell the one he had crowned was still shaky. Two of his crew had to help him onto his horse. Johnson's face was a picture of disgust over the fruitless exercise.

Clint would trail this group out of town for a ways to make sure they were headed back to their own ranch. The next couple of days would probably give Johnson enough time to either cool off or plan a counterattack. Once Clint was sure the Johnson crew was headed home, he returned to the stable. Since Joe knew the people from the last trip when he had repaired the Kansas settler's wagons, he was asked to go out to the Rio

Pecos campsite to alert everyone about possible trouble. Clint then packed enough gear to camp out near the Johnson Ranch. The pine-tree covered mountains up above the ranch complex would give a good vantage point for his spyglass.

On the second day of spying on the ranch complex, he spotted some activity. Clint counted ten armed riders headed back to Santa Fe. This could be Johnson's response, so Clint had to get around Santa Fe and in position to help at the Rio Pecos group's campsite. His traders had brought women, children and old people for this major trading get-together. Clint must prevent disaster from falling on these good, unsuspecting people.

Clint positioned himself about half a mile from the campsite. He selected a good bluff with a well-worn horse trail for rapid escape, but also a clear view of the paths leading up to the traders' campsite. Joe Black must have gotten the word to the Rio Pecos people, for the guards were out on the perimeter. Then he spotted Joe Black. He had stayed with the camp and was doing his job of repairing wagons, greasing wheels, and checking horseshoes.

The Johnson riders were only a couple of hours behind Clint. They were spotted about a mile away. He could tell that the raiding party was sending out two scouts out front. This would give Clint enough time to move around behind the Johnson riders as they waited for the report from their scouts. Clint had moved in rather close by the time the two scouts reported back to the other riders.

Clint could not hear the discussion, but a plan was being drawn out on the ground with everyone circled around. The group then broke up into three parts. Two riders headed out on either side of the traders camp and six men tied their horses and started sneaking on foot toward the camp. It would take these men at least 30 minutes to reach their goal. If Clint could warn the camp when the men on foot were about halfway there and coming without their horses, his outlying Mexican guards should be able to control the four bandits that were moving in on the sides. And then, it would be time to deal with the six men on foot. Clint was amazed that this group of would-be killers did not leave a guard on their horses. Clint slipped up to the tied horses, dropped off their saddles and turned them loose. Then, it took only two warning shots to scatter the horses and alert the camp. Clint heard some immediate gunfire as he moved to higher ground. Reaching a ledge, his spyglass was able to spot two loose saddle horses without riders. Additional gunfire was coming from the far right of the camp. Then Clint could see the two Johnson riders trying to escape the gunfire of three Mexican guards. They did not make it.

The six men on foot were backtracking toward where they had left their horses.

This would be some long shooting for Clint, but a few shots should hold the retreating gunmen. Clint was just about to squeeze off a shot when he saw two more of his Mexican guards circling around the six men on foot. The six Johnson men sprayed a few shots toward the two riders and were answered with a barrage of gunfire from all sides. Only two of the six men were standing when the smoke cleared. Clint looking on from his hidden vantage point could see that his guards had everything under control. No need to interfere or even be recognized. He sneaked back to town and retreated to his loft.

He would just wait to see what stories were spun about the ill-planned raid and the heroic defense put up by the Rio Pecos Compound people. It didn't take long for the Mexican guards to bring in the two captured gunmen and turn them over to the Territory Marshall's office.

When Joe got back to the livery stable, the story he told was already beginning to grow. Not only was it reported that more than a dozen armed men attacked the Rio Pecos campsite, but no mention of the fact that over half the men had been on foot and that the camp had been forewarned and was waiting for the attackers.

Joe also told Clint that one of the men that had roughed Clint and Joe up was among those killed. Clint observed a bit of satisfaction in Joe's face. At least there was occasional justice in the world.

Chapter 9

Joe Black was aptly named. He was a blacksmith, as big as a barn and of African descent. His family had been transported from Spain to Mexico City by the Spanish Army when he was a very small boy. His life in Mexico had mirrored his father's. The skills of the forge seemed to come naturally. Although his family had been slaves to the Spanish Army and later the Mexican Army, the skillset of a blacksmith provided them a certain independence. When the Mexican Army moved up the Rio Grande Valley to Santa Fe, Joe Black's family was taken along to care for the horses, wagons and guns. When the Mexican Army pulled back out of New Mexico Territory, many of the Mexican and Spanish families stayed.

The fairly rapid retreat of the Mexican Army had left a lot behind. This included this blacksmith family and their whole set up and tools. Since ownership was mostly determined by force and grit, for several years Joe's dad ran an independent stable. However, within a few years, one of the powerful families took over their stable and blacksmith holdings and they were once again working for a landholder. This new master had become more and more cruel and demanding. Joe's nights were constantly interrupted with orders to repair wagons, saddle horses and even deliver mounts before sun up.

After three of the most abusive gun hands were found with their throats cut, gossip had it that these men had harassed the wrong people. Since Joe was in an ideal position to observe the comings and goings of most people in Santa Fe, he began to see a pattern developing with the Pecos River compound people.

When these people came to town it seemed to coincide with the presence of the odd hide-trader. There was no obvious sign that the Rio Pecos group was with or even knew of this man. It also seemed another coincidence that connected with any punishment dealt out to offending gunmen, the presence of this dark, dirty hide-trader was noted.

Joe's keen eye for horses and guns told him that in spite of appearance, this trader was well-armed, and he was riding one of the finest horses in the area. The trader had several horses that were all of excellent breeding. The obvious health of the horses indicated that they were receiving good care. Contrarily, the horses were never brushed, giving them a shabby look which served to mislead any judgement of their quality. One time Joe had offered to rub down the trader's horse after a late arrival. The trader had declined, saying it might spoil the horse. Declining the offer to make his horse look good confirmed Joe's opinion that the trader wanted his appearance to stay low-key and unnoticed.

Late one evening, Joe was rousted out of bed by one of the owner's top guns, one of the meanest of the lot. Even his own group seemed to fear him and gave him extra space. He went by the name of Big Jake. Now even though Joe was a very big man, this Jake was even bigger. Joe had seen Big Jake take on three cowpokes and beat them unmercifully. Thus, Joe tried to avoid Big Jake, or at least not make him mad. This night it was clear that Big Jake was in a foul mood and looking for an excuse to beat someone.

So when Big Jake spotted the hide-trader's horse in the stable, he demanded that Joe saddle him. Joe tried to explain that the horse wasn't his and that the owner could call for it at any time. This refusal set Big Jake off. A gun barrel upside Joe's head put him on his knees. Then a cruel, vicious kick to the head just about put Joe's lights out. He was down on all fours trying to get his senses back when Big Jake gave him a rib-cracking kick into the stomach and chest. He rolled over to see a knife flash in the lantern light before all went black.

Joe did not know how long he was unconscious, but now the sun was just rising. That meant about five or six hours. It was a Sunday morning and no one had come by the stable as far as Joe could tell.

He slowly got to his feet and staggered over to the water trough. The cold water helped to clear his head, but the pain in his ribs and the large lump and cut beside his head was almost unbearable.

He could not bring the events of the last night back into focus. He knew that Big Jake had beaten him terribly and the flashing of a big knife blade was somewhere in his memory. Joe closed up the stable and hit his bed. Maybe a day of rest would help him to sort out the events of the night.

Monday morning found Joe in tremendous pain, so he sneaked down to the back door of the doctor's office. The doctor's horse and buggy had been under Joe's care for several years. They had an open, mutual respect for each other. After some extensive repair work and some pain killers, Joe was at least mobile. The doctor was discreet and did not ask questions. While broken ribs had not caused any other damage inside the body, Joe would have to avoid lifting for several weeks. The head concussion could possibly be a more serious concern, but only time would tell if any brain damage was involved. The pain killers would help him to endure the pain, although he was warned to take it lightly, because when you try to stop, it can be rough.

Later that afternoon, the Mexican-looking hide-trader came back to Joe's stable driving one of Joe's wagons and horses. Joe's head was hurting him so much that conversation was unwelcome. The hide-trader put Joe's wagon and horses away and saddled up his horse. Then the trader went about fixing up the stable, feeding the stock, plus putting down new straw in the area where Joe had been beaten. Then the mysterious character disappeared. Joe saw a fresh bucket of water beside his door, plus a loaf of bread.

Over the next couple of weeks, the townspeople came and went, fetching their own mounts as they recognized Joe's poor condition. The hide-trader came by every few days, fed the stock, brought Joe food and water, plus did any repair work that was urgent. He would appear without noise, swiftly complete the tasks and disappear. His speed and efficiency was remarkable.

Twice the landlord had come looking for Big Jake and complained about Joe's lack of work. Joe was threatened with eviction if he didn't get his act together quickly. By the third week following his terrible beating, the blacksmith was partially back to work. Though the doctor was reasonably sure that no permanent damage had been done, he cautioned Joe to continue light work for several more weeks.

Joe was taking his morning meal at one of the local back street cafés, a great place to hear the local gossip. The word was out that Big Jake had not been seen for three weeks. Most of the locals that frequented Maria's Café were very pleased, but worried. The sheriff was really checking out everyone that had had a run-in with Big Jake. Nearly everyone in Maria's Café had been harassed at one time or another by this hateful gunman. The sheriff had narrowed down Big Jake's movements so that Joe's stable was the last place he was known to have visited. The owner had told the sheriff that Big Jake had been sent to the stable to get the best mount for an early morning trip. Big Jake did not make that trip as far as anyone could tell.

Joe confessed that Big Jake had come to the stable, demanded a mount, and when Joe could not satisfy him, Big Jake had beat him unconscious. Joe didn't know what happened after that because he didn't come around for five or six hours, and by then Jake and his horse were gone. Joe told the sheriff that Big Jake had been in a foul mood and was looking for trouble. Maybe he found more than he could handle. The doctor had sided with Joe by telling the sheriff that Joe was so badly beaten that he could not have moved Big Jake or hauled him away.

The sheriff and the stable owner were not completely buying the story, but both knew Big Jake's hot temper and his bad moods. Many of the owner's other gunmen and wranglers were not sorry to have some relief from the oppressive style of Big Jake. The sheriff's presence was of real concern to Joe – especially, after uncovering the large blood stains where he had been beaten. It was the same spot that the hide-trader had spread a lot of clean new straw. This was on his mind when he found the hide-trader stacking the stable stall's manure on that area of the barn floor. It would seem more logical to clean the stalls by throwing the manure into the center of the walkway. The coincidence was too much. A mutual look passed between Joe and this strange hide-trader, and in the meeting of their eyes, they understood. No additional discussion was needed between them and none was asked for or provided. Joe's strength was returning, so he pitched in to finish cleaning the stalls, put down new straw and feed the livestock without a word between them. The giant pile of waste straw and manure was left. It would completely mask the blood stain and prevent the inspection of a curious sheriff or owner.

As Joe's health returned, he saw less and less of the trader. His horse would show up in Joe's stable, sometimes even two horses, and would be left there for several days. They often showed signs of hard riding, so Joe took it as his responsibility to tend the trader's mounts whenever they appeared. It was a little unnerving in that this rider could come and go, trade horses and re-saddle without disturbing Joe. It was probably a little due to the light dose of pain killers the doctor was providing. The doctor told Joe he would gradually reduce the dose and he should be completely on his own within the next couple of weeks. Joe's headaches were reducing in frequency and intensity. Even his ribs were a lot less troublesome, so that most of the blacksmith and stable chores could now be done without too much pain. His strength was almost back to normal.

Even so, things were not going well between him and the imposing owner of the stable. The demands for wagon repairs, gun modifications, the delivery of horses to the rancher's gunmen and trail crews, plus making a profit for the owner as the town's blacksmith were constant. He had become a slave again to a domineering landlord. The brief period of freedom between the time the Mexican Army had abandoned him and the takeover of his stable by the rich rancher and landowner had revealed desires in him that could not be quieted. Each day of domination became more and more unbearable.

Joe was beginning to believe that this quiet hide-trader was the protector of the Rio Pecos Compound. He had seen too many times when the people of Pecos were avenged or protected when the presence or some signs of the trader appeared in his stable. But Joe kept all of this to himself.

It seemed that a final chapter to Joe's blacksmith life was being written by his landlord.

He showed up one day, accompanied by the sheriff, and presented Joe with an eviction notice. The sheriff told Joe that since he was without any means of livelihood or support, he should move on shortly. The landlord would bring his own blacksmith crew from his ranch next week and he expected that Joe would vacate the premises within the seven days. The sheriff made it clear that if any of the tools or equipment were missing, he would be a wanted man.

Blacksmithing was the only trade Joe had known since he was a young boy working beside his father. Without tools or a place to work, he was faced with fear for his own survival. This would be the first time in his entire life that he was without a job or even a place to live. Even when he was a slave, housing and food had been provided. The fear of this unknown felt like a stranglehold to him. His mind would not focus. He went through the routine of each day, but still could not come up with a plan of action. The deadline was drawing closer and this only caused his panic to deepen. The headaches returned, the shortness of breath at night and a sense of despair was sapping his strength. It was just then that he came face to face with the smelly, quiet hide-trader. A gushing plea for help jumped out of Joe's mouth as they stood in the middle of the barn pathway beside the huge mound of manure. Joe could not contain himself as he presented the serious state of his affairs. He had always considered himself a dignified self-contained person. It was not in his character to ask for help or complain. Joe did not recognize this uncharacteristic release of hopelessness, anger, fear and desperation. It left him completely drained. He stood before this complete stranger without any defenses. The hide-trader had not said a word, but had just waited until Joe had completed exhausted himself.

Then a hand was presented for a firm, but friendly and knowing contact. "Joe, you can call me Clint. May I call you Joe? The Rio Pecos people need a good citizen, and if you would provide us with blacksmithing, we could sure use your services. I understand you are in a position that would allow you to relocate."

Chapter 10

Client knew that the surveyor that had falsified those papers for Claude Johnson against the Rio Pecos Compound must be found or this problem could rise up again. The railroad had set up a field office in Santa Fe, but their main front line office was up near the Raton Pass and another one was in a trail town called Las Vegas. It only took a couple of days of observing the Santa Fe office to identify some railroad workers and join them at cards. Clint soon learned that the chief surveyor was named Charlie Atkinson. His office was in the big, new hotel that had just been completed in Las Vegas. It became rather clear that these field survey workers did not trust or care for their top man. Atkinson never went into the field himself. He often changed the field notes and then the field crews would be sent back out to change their placement of survey monuments. Atkinson spent lots of money, too much for the salary that a railroad or government surveyor could earn. His lavish lifestyle and association with the rich landholders was not missed by these hardworking field crews. Clint learned that Atkinson frequently came to Santa Fe to meet with Claude Johnson. The field surveyors were sure that Atkinson and Johnson were long-time friends from back east, maybe St. Louis.

The construction of the westward rail lines had reached Abilene, Kansas. Stockyards were being built there near the rail head. Train service from St. Louis and Chicago to Abilene was anticipated by next year. Clint had heard a rumor from one of the Bond Ranch workers that Sr. Bond was planning a big sheep drive to Abilene next summer. The price for wool, hides, and mutton was expected to be almost double what the merchants were paying in Durango.

Clint hung around Santa Fe keeping a lookout for Atkinson. He was hoping to see the meeting between Johnson and Atkinson. It was not yet clear that Johnson had completely given up his quest to acquire the Rio Pecos Ranch. Johnson's loss of so many men during the raid on the Rio Pecos trading camp would have stopped most land-grabbers. Soon afterwards, Johnson had been able to get two of his men out of jail. No one from Rio Pecos had come to testify about the raid, so the judge had dismissed the case. Clint noticed several new gun hands around Mr. Johnson every time he appeared in Santa Fe. These could be just replacements. Mr. Johnson's gunmen were having a rather bad year.

The latest two that had disappeared were the ones sent to move Joe Black out of the livery stable. Mr. Johnson knew that his men had done their job because Joe had been laid up for over a week. The blacksmith did eventually pack up and leave Santa Fe, but the two gunmen had not been seen again.

Johnson's men now ran the stable and the Mexican hide-trader had been run out of his loft room above the stable. These kind of stories circulated around and they served Clint's needs just fine. There was no need to correct the tales with facts.

He found a run-down shack with stable stalls on the edge of town. The owner was more than glad to rent it for a year. It was so rough that no one else would live in it. The shack and Clint's hide-trader appearance fit perfectly.

A little carpenter work, new bedding and security locks made the place just right for his needs. The horse stalls and lot opened onto a back alley, whereas the front of the house was on a narrow, winding street . . . not much more than a dirt path.

Clint was loafing near the general store when one of the surveyor workers passed him accompanying well-dressed gentlemen. This had to be Charlie Atkinson, the chief surveyor from the Las Vegas office. Clint hurried around the back streets so he could be in position to watch the meeting between Johnson and Atkinson. He would get as close as he dared. Even if he could not hear the conversation, watching their faces would help.

So, Clint filled himself a plate of food, grabbed a beer and then joined a table of three other working-type men. One man was even dirtier than Clint and smelled worse, too, so Clint fit right in. It was almost an hour before Atkinson came into the saloon and headed straight to Johnson's special table. During the hour of waiting, Clint had traded seats a couple of times. His position now gave him an excellent view of Johnson's table. Clint bought his table a round of beer. This would keep the table members in place. None of these working men would think of leaving a free beer.

The meeting between Johnson and Atkinson looked very serious. Johnson had asked the other players at his table to leave and to give him some privacy. While the discussion was way too low for Clint to hear anything, their expressions were serious and grew mean looking. Claude Johnson was shaking his head no several times as Atkinson would lean into the conversation, apparently asking Johnson for something or for him to do something. Clint could see some fear and some anger in Johnson's face. Atkinson's face was not as visible, but he was definitely pushing the agenda. Clint could tell the meeting was nearing its end, so he slowly moved out. He wanted to see how many men were with these two, and try to memorize their looks.

Clint counted at least eight men acting as guards for Johnson and Atkinson. Four of the eight were locals that he had seen with Johnson before. The other four were new faces. At least two of these new faces were definitely experienced gun hands given their expensive gear. They had the look of confident bodyguards, a step up from the gunmen that Johnson had been hiring. Charlie Atkinson must have enough money or backing to put on such a show, and have Johnson cater to him. Johnson was a powerful man in Santa Fe circles.

Atkinson and Johnson went to Santa Fe's best hotel near the market square. The guards spread out around the hotel. The two top guns were inside with Atkinson. It was difficult for Clint to stand watch on the hotel being so close to the market square. A lot of his people were still trading and buying supplies around the square.

The next observation spot for Clint would be the land office. If Atkinson and Johnson were continuing their pursuit of the Rio Pecos ranch, they would probably come there to verify their claim against the ranch. It was almost noon the next day before Atkinson went to the land office. He was in the office for only a very short period of time. The look on his face as he came out was that of an unhappy man. His stride was deliberate and angry as he returned to the hotel, two top guns by his sides all the way.

Clint did notice that one of Atkinson's other guards had been posted up the street from the land office. This gent was probably told to report anyone going in or out of the land title recording office. Clint would like to know if a new notice had been posted at the land office, but the risk was too high to look now.

Clint's check on the traders' camp revealed that his people were packing up for their trip back to Rio Pecos. From his distant perch and with his spyglass, he could see that everyone was in good spirits, wagons loaded and all the sheep sold. Just to be cautious, he would watch over the wagon train until it passed through the Gloriata Pass, and then come back to monitor this Atkinson fellow.

Over the next couple of days, Clint made the rounds to Johnson's ranch overlook, then back to the Golden Mint saloon, including a check on Atkinson's bodyguards near the market square hotel. Johnson and Atkinson had settled into a regular routine of big eating, gambling and pretty women. They had either decided to forget the Rio Pecos deal or they were entertaining themselves as they waited for something or some else.

The lookout for the land office finally abandoned his post. This gave Clint a chance to slip inside for a quick inspection.

Clint wasn't surprised to see an updated notice referencing a new survey by Charlie Atkinson. The claim stated that the original survey of five years ago had been in error, thus the major portion of the land deeded to Brad Mason and Cliff Martinez was not valid. This new survey had the buildings and water well area of Rio Pecos Compound belonging to Claude Johnson and company. The registered land surveyor, Charlie Atkinson, would personally have to testify at the land office hearings next month. Clint's task would be to prevent Atkinson's testimony. The word from the survey workers had Atkinson returning to Las Vegas to retrieve the new survey documents, plus a copy of the old mistaken survey. This claim that his old survey was located in Las Vegas was probably the heart of the fraud. Clint knew his real land survey was filed with the Santa Fe land office.

Clint decided that a trip to Las Vegas was the best course of action. If it came down to a confrontation between him and Atkinson, it would be better if it was outside of Santa Fe. Clint would take two horses. That would put him in Las Vegas a couple of days ahead of Atkinson and his guards. Clint took two completely different dress outfits, plus two saddles and gear. He might have to play more than one role to protect his identity in Santa Fe.

The trip north on the Santa Fe Trail went swiftly and without a hitch. He avoided three freight loads headed south as well as several groups of riders. He had taken only enough time on the trail to detour to his ranch house to switch horses and get some extra clothing. He slipped in and out quietly, but two of his Mexican guards revealed themselves. They reported that everything was under control at the compound. Even the blacksmith had arrived.

Clint arrived in Las Vegas early in the afternoon wearing the dress and gear of a wealthy rancher. That gave him time to locate Atkinson's office. If he could get inside the office and scout out the layout before Atkinson arrived, maybe he could develop a plan. He would make conversation about the future of the railroad and its route through the area south of Las Vegas. The two office workers were very eager to present their plans to Clint. They were showing off some independence with Atkinson out of the office. A question about the Mora land grant and the availability of land for sale prompted them to display a large map. Clint could see several corrections on the southern boundary. These surveys were very familiar to Clint, because he had worked on them five years earlier. The land south of the Mora grant was now identified as the C. Johnson and Company holdings with B. Mason crossed off. Clint then saw the footnote he was looking for; a survey notebook number and date.

Bound survey notebooks were the official records. They were usually cross-referenced by map coordinates, dates of survey and book number. Clint identified the two books that would tell the story; his original survey five years ago, and the new survey book that was completed just last year. The office worker then pulled out a larger map that covered the area between Las Vegas and Raton Pass. He proudly pointed out some land that was available for sale. Mr. Atkinson would be back in a couple of days. He would be the contact if Clint wanted to buy land up that way. Clint acted very interested and took some notes about directions and landmarks. He let the office help believe that he was going up there to look over the area. While Clint was busy looking over the Raton area maps, some angry ranchers came into the survey office. This left Clint alone with the maps during the heated discussion with the five ranchers. The ranchers were contending that they had bought some land from Sr. Bond four years ago. The title was being challenged so they wanted to see the original survey. The office staff unlocked the big glass case that held the original survey books. They pulled the two books that covered the two different dates the ranchers were complaining about.

Clint could clearly see the new book that covered his revised land area survey. When the group was in a very intense discussion with everyone bent over the other table in the next room, Clint did a swift shuffle of books and removed three. Clint then saw two older survey books lying on a side table along with one new book. A quick look showed him that another fraud was being prepared. Clint put these books back into the glass case and left one of the other books on the side work table.

When he excused himself, the office workers only looked up briefly from their heated discussion. He promised to come back if the land up north looked any good. Then he headed north out of town. After a short distance, he pulled off the road and circled around the town to where he had left his other horse. A change of clothes and horse made a completely different man out of Clint. He then moved to a position to watch the trail from the south and the survey office.

If he could find out what land dispute these ranchers were having, maybe their problem could mask his plan. It was almost sundown when the ranchers came stomping out of the survey office. It must have been quitting time because the office workers locked up and left almost immediately after. The angry ranchers headed down the street to a large café that was attached to a hotel. Clint made his way down from his lookout perch and entered the café. He picked a small table beside the men he had seen at the survey office. They did not give him any notice. He was just another dusty trail hand.

Their discussion was no trouble to follow. They were both angry and loud. Someone was trying to steal the land they had purchased from the Bond land grant. They even openly threatened to burn down the survey office. Two more men came over to the large table to join in on the discussion. Everyone was in agreement that something was crooked about land dealing in this region. It was clear that most of these men had planned on getting rich when the railroads purchased the right-of-way through their ranches. The problem was identifying who was behind this fraud. The railroads could be ripping off everyone, the government land grant surveyors could be crooked, or even the big Spanish land grant holders could be double dealing. This open display of anger would be the perfect cover for Clint to make a raid on the survey office.

Late that night, Clint broke into the survey office and ransacked the place. A selection of survey books was taken, mostly those that covered the lands of the angry ranchers. It had to look like a revenge raid by that group so that Clint's missing survey book would just be lost along with the others. The last piece of the puzzle was the dropping of a couple of the rancher's survey books in the livery stable where the ranchers were keeping their horses.

Clint headed back to Rio Pecos. If this did not derail Atkinson and Johnson, then a more drastic action would be forthcoming.

Chapter 11

A month of hard work at the ranch took Clint's mind off the title hearing pending in Santa Fe. Joe Black, the blacksmith, had become a welcome member of the community. Almost the entire Kansas settler group had pitched in to build Joe a set of quarters next to the big ranch barn that was serving as a blacksmith shop and repair place. When Clint introduced himself as Cliff Martinez, there was a small smile on Joe's face, but not a single question. Clint could tell that Joe recognized him as the Mexican hide-trader, but not a word was said. It was a secret between them. They both benefited from this arrangement, so why dig any deeper?

Clint could not put off the trip to Santa Fe any longer. He must find out if Johnson and Atkinson were going to carry through on the challenge to his ownership of Rio Pecos. Arriving at his old house in Santa Fe with three horses was a bit showy, but he might need the extra mounts if things went sour.

After cleaning up his place, he made the rounds to see who was in town. There was no sign of Atkinson or his guards. Johnson's table at the Golden Mint was empty, but reserved. The land office still had the notice for his ranch title challenge posted on the board. The hearing date was one week away.

A trip out to look over Johnson's ranch complex provided a little information. He spotted at least three of Atkinson's bodyguards around the bunkhouse and on Johnson's front porch. It looked as though Johnson was holding up in his own house or maybe was being confined by Atkinson's men. Clint thought back to the first meeting he had witnessed between the two men. He could guess that Johnson wanted to back out of the hearing and Atkinson was making sure that Johnson would carry through on his part. Clint returned to Santa Fe anticipating the arrival of Atkinson. The loss of the survey records and the additional disputes up north might convince Atkinson this particular fraud wasn't worth the risk. But the hope that this whole thing would just blow over was dashed the next day with the arrival of Atkinson with half a dozen gunmen.

The very next day, Johnson came into town with the three Atkinson men, plus at least four of his own men. It definitely looked like Johnson was being escorted and not just guarded. The meetings were held in the hotel, so Clint could not observe the reactions between the two men. This setup was calling for a little more persuasion or pressure.

Clint took his crossbow, some rags and grease and headed out to Johnson's ranch. A close overlook of the complex located a target. A large stack of hay was piled against the side of the largest barn. The tree line was close enough so that Clint's crossbow could launch a flaming arrow into the haystack from tree cover. Wrapping a greasy rag around an arrow took only a few minutes. Getting the grease to ignite took some effort, but finally it caught fire. The long arching arrow hit its mark. Within minutes, the flames had spread from the haystack to the barn. Clint made his way back out of cover to his horse and returned to Santa Fe.

To get the full benefit from his plan, Clint needed to get a message to Johnson about his barn fire before a rider could get here from his ranch. A message left at the Golden Mint bar would do the trick. But it was not very easy to get close enough to Johnson's favorite barmaid to slip a note onto her tray. Clint had to wait for the right moment and he knew that time was running out. When a drunk started hassling the barmaid, she became fully occupied dealing with the disturbance. That was what Clint was waiting for. A quick step past the lady's tray and the note lay in open sight when she got back. She saw the paper immediately and gave it to the bartender.

The note was then sent by foot over to the hotel. It took only a few minutes before several men showed up to quiz the bartender and barmaid. A lot of the saloon customers started moving out of the place. This questioning was getting too intense and the crowd could feel the tension. Clint joined a small group that made its way out onto the front porch and then dispersed. Clint moved on down the street to the general store. He made himself busy buying a few items, but stayed close enough to the front windows to watch the hotel front entrance. It was almost no time before a rider came at full run to the hotel. Even at this distance, Clint could see black soot all over his clothes. He must have helped fight the barn fire before coming to town with the report.

It did not take long before Johnson and Atkinson appeared on the hotel front porch. There was an energetic exchange, but it was obvious that Johnson had had enough. A few minutes later, horses were brought up from the stable. Johnson and his men saddled up and rode out of town toward his ranch. Atkinson was left standing on the hotel front porch with his men waiting for instructions. The whole group finally moved down the boardwalk to the hotel.

Within 30 minutes Atkinson came out and barked some orders. Several of the men had had horses at the hotel hitching rail. These men mounted up and headed down the street to the livery stable. Within minutes a buggy was brought to the hotel along with enough horses for everyone. Suitcases were brought out of the hotel and loaded onto the buggy. Finally Atkinson left town with his gang in tow. Clint had high hopes that this exodus of the land title challengers, those who were challenging title to his land was a victory for him and for his village. But, he would have to wait for the announced hearing in a few days before he would know for sure.

In the meantime he had some free time to work on his rented quarters and maybe to gamble. It was hard for him to work inside his house when a good game of cards was there waiting for his skills. Working on someone else's building was not much inspiration. Upgrading one's own property was much more rewarding. The owner of his rental house obviously had not put much into it himself.

The very next day, the owner spotted Clint at the bar and invited him to join their card game. The game was friendly enough, but the landlord was not a very good card player. It was soon apparent why his house had not been maintained. The owner was losing his money at cards, so much so that one of the other players at the table held a promissory note on the very house Clint was renting.

This was revealed when a player put a promissory note in with the other liens against Clint's residence. The owner then offered to sell the house to Clint to satisfy the note if only Clint would give him $100 for the title. One of the players jokingly cautioned Clint that there may be other liens against that old house and they all agreed that the rundown house wasn't worth $100. Clint, in a good-natured way, accepted the offer and bought a round of drinks. Everyone at the table signed as witnesses. Clint could tell that the players thought their friend, the landlord, had gotten the best of the Mexican hide-trader.

For the next couple of days, Clint was busy fixing up the old house. Now that it was his, the efforts changed from work to pure fun. It was all in the attitude; ownership does something to the mind.

Clint took the property title papers over to the land office. He needed a good excuse to look around to find the current state of the challenge to Rio Pecos without casting any suspicions on himself. The title clerk was all business when Clint gave him the handwritten title papers. This type of transaction was common. In fact, Clint was surprised that the liens against the property had been recorded.

The clerk had a separate book for recording liens and lien satisfactions and the change was handled very smoothly. Then Clint was asked who would hold the new clear title to the house. Clint asked if the new owner had to be present to record the title in his name. He was told that that was not necessary if Clint knew his legal name and address. Clint then gave Cliff Martinez as the new owner. He would be renting the house from Sr. Martinez of Rio Pecos. The clerk immediately recognized the name and went over to the bulletin board and retrieved the hearing notice. He told Clint that Johnson and Atkinson had dropped the claim against the Cliff Martinez and Brad Mason ranch down on the Rio Pecos. The clerk hadn't believed that their claim would hold up because that very ranch had been surveyed by a government surveyor over five years ago and recorded in this very office.

Chapter 12

Clint headed out of Santa Fe on the trail north to Española. The rumor of a major sheep drive from the Bond ranch next spring to the railhead in Kansas was on his mind. Clint's herd would need a major culling by then. The count could be as high as 30,000 sheep. The trail nearest the Rio Grande would work out best. It would keep him a good distance from the Johnson Ranch, as he wanted to stay clear of that place until some time had passed.

Sr. Bond was very gracious and friendly as usual. Clint knew that Bond had made good money on their last deal, so there was considerable interest in another arrangement. Sr. Bond was planning a trip to Abilene, Kansas, with a large sheep herd, and three other ranchers had already agreed to join the drive. With Clint's 30,000 head, the total count would be close to 250,000 sheep. It would take between 120 and 130 days to make such a trip if everything went on schedule. This pace would keep the weight on the sheep and hopefully keep loss at a minimum. Sheep could be driven faster, but the costs went up quickly. Sr. Bond offered the same options as last time. This time he would pay upfront at least six cents per head or Clint and his men could just join the drive and sell their own sheep in Kansas. Either arrangement was acceptable to the Bond Ranch.

The extra men and herders would provide more protection, but Sr. Bond would be pleased with more risk for the greater profit if Clint would sell his herd before the start of the drive.

And then Sr. Bond offered another option. One of the ranches that wanted to join the drive was up the Santa Fe Trail north of Las Vegas. If Clint would drive his herd north and join with that herd, then the two could pass through the Raton Pass and join the other three herds north of it. Then all five herds could travel due east to the railheads and stockyards in Abilene.

Sr. Bond was planning on taking his flock along with one other herd from Española up the Rio Grande Valley to join a third group near Taos, then they would cross over the high ridge to the plateau just north of Raton Pass.

The rancher who was north of Las Vegas was planning on making the trip north through the Raton Pass alone. But he had experienced a number of raids, so he was selling out all his sheep. If Clint would join his drive, he knew it would make it a lot safer for all.

Previously, Sr. Bond had been quite impressed with Clint's Mexican guards. He wondered if they were still available. Clint thought that that arrangement would have to be worked out with the guards directly.

Sr. Bond told Clint about the barn fire at the Johnson Ranch over south east of him. The report was that it had not been determined if it was arson. Sr. Bond did not like Claude Johnson, but barn fires disturbed everyone. It seems Mr. Johnson had acquired his ranch under mysterious circumstances. The previous owner, with his only son, had traveled to St. Louis to visit relatives and they never came back. A few months later, Johnson showed up with deed transfer documents that were signed and witnessed in St. Louis. The previous owner did not have any living relatives left in the area, so the deal was not questioned. But Sr. Bond had been fairly close to the original owner, so the sale really surprised him. The rancher and Sr. Bond had even talked about some joint ventures to expand their holdings. Over the years, they had worked hard together to improve their herds and protect their land. The owner had expressed that his son would marry, have children and carry on their ranch into the future. The two old land holders had spent many fun hours over good wine discussing the future for both of them. In contrast, Mr. Johnson was not much of a rancher. His buildings were getting run down, his flock was not well tended nor was there any attempt to cull the herd for improvement. Mr. Johnson spent most of his time in Santa Fe partying, and while he kept a lot of gunmen on his payroll, there were not many ranch hands or herders.

Clint decided he would send a message back to Sr. Bond as to which option his people wanted to take. A lot depended on the choices of the Mexican guards. Without their extra guns, Clint would not want to take the route north to Raton Pass.

The trip back to Santa Fe would pass take him through two or three of the Indian areas. Sr. Bond had suggested that he stop and visit with a Juan Cruz in the San Juan Pueblo. The Cruz family had done a lot of adobe building for the Bond Ranch. Sr. Bond had heard that the Cruz family was on the outs with the current Indian leaders and was looking for work somewhere else. Apparently one of the Cruz girls had married a buck from the San Ildenfonso Pueblo against the San Juan tribal leader's advice. An arranged marriage had been planned between the tribal leader's son and Juan Cruz's daughter. The young bride was having a hard time with her new mother-in-law and the village people in general.

To show the family how much the San Juan tribal leaders disapproved, Juan Cruz was prohibited from participating in the annual community dances. This was very hurtful and shameful for Juan and his family.

Clint had mentioned to Sr. Bond his need for a good adobe mason. Bond thought Juan Cruz and his extended family might take the job for a few years to let things cool down in his own village. Cruz and his family were excellent masons. Cruz's mother, wife, and at least one daughter were also outstanding potters.

The ride into the San Juan Pueblo was a little eerie. Clint was riding a large and beautiful horse outfitted with top quality saddle and gear and he was also well armed as everyone could see. His first few questions in Spanish as to the whereabouts of the Cruz family were answered with local language and were no help. Clint finally spotted a young boy mixing mud for adobe bricks. A few questions about making brick cleared the air. The young boy's Spanish was very good and he easily gave Clint directions to Juan Cruz's house.

Clint's greeting at the house included the fact that Sr. Bond had suggested he come to see

Juan. Clint was invited into the house and Juan introduced himself. After a brief review of what Sr. Bond had told him, Clint said that his village needed some good adobe masons to build several homes and community buildings. When Clint identified the Rio Pecos Compound as the village, Juan's eyes gave a brief flicker and a slight smile. Juan had heard the stories about Rio Pecos. He had also met many of the Rio Pecos traders at the Santa Fe market square. Their Rio Pecos blankets were known to be some of the best in the region.

Juan Cruz then retold a story that he had heard from his father and grandfather. Many generations ago his tribe used to mine special clays on the banks of the Rio Pecos. These clays were said to be the best that could be found for making pottery. His ancestors had made a name for themselves by producing clay pots from these special clays. His grandfather had told many stories of his family mining these clays and bringing them back to their pueblo for sale and trade.

The Spaniards drove the Indians out of the Rio Pecos Valley almost 200 years ago. A large adobe house was built in the valley to house the Spanish soldiers. There was a well nearby that his grandfather said the Indians had dug to work the clays. Later the Mexican Army prohibited the Indians from leaving their designated lands. This had cut off any access to the clay mines years and years ago. While Juan was sure of these stories, very few other people in his village had even heard them. If his grandfather had not continued the tales, Juan would not be aware of this history. He then showed Clint a pot that was claimed to have been made of the Rio Pecos clays. It was beautiful and graceful and had endured the usage these many years. The seal on the bottom was his family's mark as far back as anyone could trace these things.

Juan Cruz said that his family would discuss these things and get word to Clint at the Santa Fe Market square sometime soon. Clint joined in a meal with the family before he headed back to Santa Fe. During his ride he enjoyed a feeling of accomplishment. If he could in some small way open up the path for the Cruz family to rediscover their past, that would feel good.

It would be a great step forward for his village if the Cruz family would bring their adobe building skills to the Rio Pecos Compound. Clint had been very disappointed that his people had not been able to build durable structures and their new buildings were nowhere near the quality of his old ranch house.

If Cruz's family ancestors had been among the building crews of his ranch house, then the buildings of Rio Pecos compound might stand long into the future. The Spaniards had conscripted many of the Indians in the area to build Spanish churches and missions, and many of these structures were still in use.

Clint's daydreaming was getting ahead of him, but it was fun to think of good times rather than today's lawless world. Riding into the dark back streets of Santa Fe had a way of bringing Clint back to reality and danger. He dismounted his horse at the end of the alley and cautiously worked his way up to his rear gate, checked to see that his locking system was intact, then led his horses into their stalls. He did not feel safe until he was inside and inspected the little traps that he always left for unwanted intruders. All was well, so he settled down for a good night's rest in his own shack. It wasn't much of a place, but it was his.

Clint would hang around Santa Fe for a few days to make sure the title challenge didn't raise its head again. This would give Juan Cruz a chance to get word to him of their decision. This type of major decision could take the Cruz family weeks or months. Since Clint would move on to the Rio Pecos ranch in a few days, he would alert his people to keep an ear open for the Cruz family decision during their regular trading trips.

Clint had also brought with him a small piece of clay that Juan Cruz thought had come from those old Rio Pecos clay mines. If he could match this clay piece with any clay deposits on his ranch, then he could get the word back to Juan. Better yet he could deliver a load of the clay to Juan's house in San Juan Pueblo. This thought made Clint anxious to get back to his ranch. He was wondering if the clay chips he had spotted for making adobe bricks were the same as this clay chip Juan had given him. It sure did look and feel the same.

Clint was making his rounds of the market square the next day when he saw the two mothers and five children of the Kansas settlers. These families had joined the preacher in his move to Santa Fe. It looked like they were begging for food. They looked both downtrodden and lost. Clint kept his distance, but he had to find out what was going on with these followers of the preacher. When they had left his ranch, they had enough supplies and money for a few months. Clint watched for a time, then followed them out of town to the traders' camp. There he saw one wagon and the two families gathered around a small cook fire. The preacher and the other wagons and horses were nowhere to be seen. These people needed help again. Clint went back to town and picked up some food and his other horses. The return trip to the camp was done casually as though he was just passing through. After the normal greetings, it soon came out that the preacher had gone on a mission trip to Durango and the gold fields. He had talked two of their teenage sons into going with him on his God-inspired venture. Shortly after they had left, their food stuff had been stolen and their wagons vandalized. Both families wanted to return to Rio Pecos. Clint would take them back in, but what about their sons and the preacher? These two families had experienced some reality and were ready to settle down and work for a living. Their sons would have to learn the hard way. Their prayers would be with them. The preacher had had much more influence on the two boys than their parents. Until the boys matured a little, it would be useless for the parents to give advice.

Clint shared the extra food with them and loaned them two horses. The saddle horses were not used to pulling a wagon, so someone would have to ride on them. The one wagon loaded with people and little else headed out toward the Rio Pecos Compound. The older children and adults took turns walking and riding the horses. It looked like a defeated and retreating army. Their spirits were broken. Their missionary zeal was gone. They were broke again and returning to their friends with the knowledge that everyone would know that they had failed on the missionary quest. However, the return of the two families was met with open arms and offers of support. Even one of the Navajo ladies brought over several loaves of freshly baked bread that had just come out of the oven. Clint was pleased to see signs of a developing community among this diverse collection of people.

Chapter 13

The summer heat had driven the sheep herds to the highest elevations. The cool, dry mountain air was perfect for both sheep and shepherds. However, the cougars and coyotes gave the shepherds some real problems, so the Mexican guards had turned hunters in the rough mountain terrain. It was hard work and took long hours, but the young gun hands seemed to enjoy the change. They had gotten a little relief when one of the men that had moved to Santa Fe returned to the herd. The fun and excitement of the big city had finally gotten a little old and very expensive for him.

The good food and clean bunkhouse of the Rio Pecos ranch was starting to look a lot better. If he was to save any money for the trip to Mexico City, he had to get out of Santa Fe. There were way too many pretty girls, poker tables and saloon bars for a young man to save any money. Some young men that had just returned to town had heard about the upcoming trail drive to Kansas. An adventure that was too good to pass up. A trail drive of three or four months could force you to save money. There would be no time or place to spend along the way. Besides, he had never been up north and was especially curious about Kansas.

Clint had gone over the options about the sheep drive early this next spring or maybe early summer. All of the Mexican young guns were in for the ride. The Basque herders also wanted to be a part of this major trip because their herds would be over-populated by spring. They also were interested in finding some good breeding rams to add to their herds.

While the Navajos were not interested in the trip to Kansas, they would like to accompany the drive north. They would gladly sell their share to Sr. Bond. Then they could split off and return to their native grazing area southwest of Durango. If they could successfully get around the big Apache territory, they would be reasonably safe. The word they had heard suggested that new U.S. Government Army units were doing a better job of keeping the peace near the Navajo land. The Hopi and Navajos were arguing over range land, but both tribes viewed sheep as a treasure, not just as meat like the Apache.

The Navajos were not particularly breed developers, so they had no trouble in Clint's planned culling of the herd. Clint wanted churro breed stock to strengthen the Basque merino sheep. The Navajos just wanted their fair share of the churro flock as to the numbers, with no concern for type or quality. They did not like the new crossbreed that Clint was developing because they required too much care. The pure churro could make-do without much protection or special care.

The shorter, finer wool of the merino was harder to weave on the coarse Navajo looms. The Navajo weavers liked the feel and the colors that the combined wools of the two types had produced. But the big looms at the Rio Pecos

Compound could not be transported easily. They would return to their old ways and use the long-haired churro sheep. They would miss the big dollars they were getting for the Basque/Navajo blankets, but longed for the old Navajo ways. The Basque men were much too pushy for their likes. The Navajos felt they had been away from their native soil too long. Their children needed to be with their own people or else they would lose their way. The Basque had almost no skill in the art of jewelry making. In fact, there were no artists in the whole Basque clan.

The Kansas settlers had put down roots, planted gardens and built themselves wood homes. Two of the well-educated settlers were running the school for those children that were allowed to attend. Only a few children were being kept from the school and most of those were the Navajos' kids. The Navajo children were the primary shepherds for the churro flocks. Their culture necessitated that everyone learn all the trades. The children were put to work as soon as they could carry out a task. Some of the young girls were making great blankets out of the fine wools. Their older parents and traditional Navajo weavers would have a hard time getting those girls to go back to the old ways. In fact, Clint had noticed some interest between two of the beautiful Navajo girls and two of his Mexican guards. It was obvious that the Navajo weavers were getting a lot more protection than the situation demanded. Clint had also noticed that these two young guards were passing off their hunting duties to some of the others.

Clint left the duty schedule up to the senior guard. The guard unit usually acted as a separate group with just general directions and an overall plan from Clint. The one remaining guard that had gone to Santa Fe came back to the Rio Pecos compound late one evening. He brought a message from some Indians on the market square. A Juan Cruz would like to accept the offer to move to Rio Pecos Compound and build adobe buildings. He was requesting some help to transport some of his family now. After they had built themselves houses, the rest of his clan would like to be moved over for two or three years at the most. If Clint could send three wagons and some protection to San Juan Pueblo, they would like to move immediately. The sooner they could get started on the buildings the better it would be. The goal would be to have their houses completed sufficiently to occupy before bad winter weather. Although the winters were not usually very severe, there could be a week or two at a time when outside work was difficult.

Clint organized a set of four wagons with one wagon meant to stay over at the Santa Fe traders' camp. They would haul wool, mutton and blankets for sale at the market square. The women and one store clerk would stay at the square with one guard to carry out the trading and the buying of supplies for the trading post. It was not surprising to Clint when the young Navajo and Mexican couple volunteered to help with the trading in Santa Fe.

The blankets had accumulated so that they filled two wagons. Joe Black had built two more wagons and repaired two of the Kansas settler's wagons to their original condition. The caravan set off to Santa Fe and San Juan Pueblo with good equipment, fresh horses and some eager guards and shoppers. Three of the Kansas men had agreed to drive wagons and help with the move. Five guards were sent. The hunting of the cougars and coyotes would have to be put on hold. The number of pelts that the hunters had brought down from the mountains surprised Clint. The Navajos had been kept busy tanning all of these hides. Some of the cougar hides were especially beautiful and they were huge. This harvest of hides off the mountain should reduce the number of attacks on the sheep grazing up there. Besides, the movement of sheep off the highest pastures would begin in a month or two.

As usual, Clint left ahead of the wagon train, keeping well off the trail and higher so he could keep watch on the wagons below as well as the trail ahead. As he was approaching the Gloriata Pass, he could see a group of Union soldiers working on the land some distance from the Santa Fe Trail. It looked like they were surveying and staking out building sites. This development would have to be investigated later. His wagon train passed near the soldiers, but made no contact.

Clint went straight to his house, changed clothes and hit the street to pick up any new rumors. The land office bulletin board did not contain any notices on Clint's property. The land office clerk did know that the U.S. Government had filed a claim on one-quarter section of land just east of the Gloriata Pass. The Union Army was going to move their soldiers out of Santa Fe. The new fort was going to be called Fort Union.

The word on the streets of Santa Fe had the cause for the move to be the lack of discipline among the Union troops. There were constant problems between drunken soldiers and the local law officers. Both the local sheriff and the regional U.S. Marshal, in turn, were having conflicts with the Army higher command. The Union Colonel wanted all charges against soldiers handled by the military system, whereas the sheriff and Marshal wanted the law-breaking soldiers judged and punished by the territorial court.

Clint moved around the market square until he spotted a few members of the Cruz family selling pottery. He asked for Juan Cruz and found out that he had gone back to the pueblo village to help pack supplies, tools, and household items they would need for two months. One of the young boys would go tell his dad that the wagons were headed out to the San Juan Pueblo.

It was three days later when Clint and the three wagons headed out to Cruz's house. All of the trading items had been offloaded either at the market square or at the traders' camp. The three wagons, three drivers and three guards went with Clint to the San Juan Pueblo.

Juan had two wagons of his own loaded and waiting. Clint had had the wagon train bring along four extra pull horses from Rio Pecos. He had inspected Juan's horses on his last visit. They were of very poor quality and little cared for. The Cruz family was very pleased to leave their horses behind for the family to use while Juan and the others were in Rio Pecos setting up their buildings.

Juan insisted that everyone spend the night, have a big meal with the whole extended family before leaving early the next morning. Since the Cruz ladies could really cook, it was a grand feast. Clint was sure the Mexican guards loved the food more than anyone else. At least they ate more than anyone else. It could also be that the lovely young Indian maids who were waiting on them had encouraged them to ask for second and third helpings. The family even put on a costumed circle dance for the affair.

The Cruz men packed the three new wagons that night with the final tie-downs completed the next morning. Seven Cruz family men and two women and three teenage boys were taking the trip. If Clint's count was right, that meant that there were at least 20 more adults and a dozen children that would join Rio Pecos later this fall. Clint would have to make arrangements to haul all these people and their belongings. In addition, Juan said he had seven horses and ten cows in total that would need herding to Rio Pecos along with the last move. The two wagons that Cruz had loaded for this trip were the only ones he owned, and he knew they were not in very good shape.

The trip back to the Santa Fe traders' camp was easily completed the next day. The following morning was spent loading the purchased supplies, packing everyone up and finally heading out to the Rio Pecos Compound. One night would be spent on the trail. Attired as a ranch owner, Clint would travel with the wagons. He wanted to tour the site where the Army was staking out the new fort. Mostly, he wanted to find out what improvements were planned for the Santa Fe

Trail coming into town from the new fort location. Sometimes these Army outposts provided camping sites for travelers, since their location was usually about a one-day easy ride from Santa Fe and Rio Pecos Compound. It would be an ideal stop-over for his people, plus it would be protected by the Army.

After the night's lay-over, the wagons headed on to the ranch and Clint detoured to the planned site for Fort Union. The soldiers had only a simple layout plan for the fort buildings and walls. The plans did indicate a small space inside the fort for visitors and wagons and a larger cleared area outside the walls. The men working at the site had no idea about the building schedules or about any improvements planned for the road back to Santa Fe.

With this information, Clint put a rush on his horse so he could catch up with the wagons. When he arrived at the compound, he laid out the area where Sr. Cruz and his clan could set up camp. He gave Juan a sketch of the proposed village expansion that he was planning. Clint would work with them tomorrow to site individual buildings, mall, street and well. A new well was to be dug at the far end of the new street. Clint had estimated a well of 30 to 40 feet deep would intercept the same aquifer that served the existing well. He had shot the elevation of water in the existing well to a spring outcrop down the slope toward the river bank. Working together, the Navajos and Basque had opened up the spring and rocked in a good watering place for the livestock. Even during the driest part of the year that spring had continued to flow.

The Pueblos got settled in that evening and were eager to start work the next morning. They went to see the clay pit that Clint had suggested for the adobe bricks. Juan was very pleased with this clay deposit. It had a lot better texture than what had been available near San Juan Pueblo. Juan quickly organized teams and everyone went to work. One crew would make bricks, one crew would haul rocks for the foundations, and another group of men would start digging footers. All were self-motivated to build new houses for themselves first. The women started to build a few mud ovens for baking. Some tents were set up for temporary housing and shelter. All the wagons were lined up with tent covers for sleeping quarters. In less than a week the Indians were completely set up in temporary camps. Foundations were being dug and rock filled for support. The need to dry the bricks until they had enough strength was the time restraint. Juan had learned that a dryer mud packed extra tight in the mold was the path to eventual speed and strength.

Some of the Kansas carpenters had pitched in to build window and door frames and cut logs for the roof support. Three big wagon loads of logs and lumber had been delivered from Bond's saw mill. Cut spikes had been bought at the Santa Fe General Store. The spikes speeded up the work of assembly compared to the old wood peg with drilled or burned holes.

The new clay deposit proved to be an excellent mud for bricks and plaster. Plus a layer of the clay deposit did match the clay type about which Juan's grandfather had told his stories. One of the Pueblo women went to work making some clay pots and firing ovens. She would have to go through the whole process before she could be sure the clay was the right type. While it worked well and was strong enough to hold its slopes during the molding process, it would be the baking process that would give the final answer.

The excitement from the surge of the new building spread throughout the whole compound. There would be three to six men and boys working on the new dug well every day without anyone asking. Juan had even picked up some help from the Kansas settlers to haul rocks and till trenches for footers.

Once the first bricks were ready for laying, the process continued from sun-up to sunset. Five homes, one bunkhouse, one workshop, a community kitchen and dining hall were all started at once. At this rate, Juan Cruz would be able to bring the rest of his clan to Rio Pecos long before winter. Juan was getting anxious to have the rest of his people experience this community building process.

Chapter 14

Rio Pecos Compound was rapidly becoming a village. The Pueblo masons were building some beautiful buildings. The clay deposit had turned out to be excellent for adobe brick. The Pueblo ladies were preparing their first batch of pots for sale at the market square. They were so proud of what they had made that it was hard for them to maintain the low profile look that was their custom. To show too much pride would bring resentment from others. It was best that your good works spoke for you, with no bragging on yourself. The recognition for something well done was someone else's choice.

The second well had been completed with good water flow. A pulley bucket and rope system had been built under a small covered area to draw the water. A second watering trough had been constructed for horses, sheep and cattle. The well was also the water source for the adobe work.

A set of corrals had been put up along with a shed anticipating the arrival of the Cruz family horses and cows. The first two families had left their wagon and tent homes to occupy the first two completed homes. Those two families had opened their doors to all the others that wanted to bunk in a real house. Both houses were full all the time. The Pueblo crew's pace was to finish about one building a week now. The roofing systems were taking somewhat longer. More logs were ordered from the sawmill. Two of the Mexican guards were more than happy to take four days off for the ride through Santa Fe to the sawmill. Clint knew the young guns would ride straight to the sawmill, then to Santa Fe, spend their money and limp back home broke. It was a pattern that these young, energetic men could do over and over without regrets. In time, they may learn better, that is if they lived that long.

It was time for Clint to have a meeting with Sr. Bond to work out the spring or early summer sheep drive. He also needed some additional intelligence about the Apache area. If the Navajos were going to return to their homeland, Clint needed to find their best pathway. Clint sure hated to see the Navajos leave Rio Pecos. They had added a lot to the community. They had taught the Pueblos, Basque and Kansas settlers their arts of weaving and jewelry making. The Pueblos were showing their skills of pottery work and adobe brick building with everyone. The Basque shepherds had found some deposits of turquoise gems up on the high range and had brought down several large stones for the Navajos to inspect. The Navajos and Pueblos were now working some of the stone into their jewelry. They were guided by the Basque shepherds and went back up the mountain to locate more good rocks. It would take some work before the Navajos would know the quality of the stones.

The meeting with Sr. Bond covered a lot of items. The drive would try to start the first full moon in June. This would give Clint one month to reach the plateau just north of the Raton Pass.

Bond's herds should be at that point after they had joined the herd near Taos Pueblo. Sr. Bond has a planned meeting in Santa Fe with the sheep owner from up north of Las Vegas. Clint should join them the first weekend in November at the Western Plaza Hotel. They could jointly refine the dates and routes of travel. Sr. Bond had a small herd headed to the Durango mining camps right then. He should have a good report on the area and the Apache situation when his men returned.

Another area of interest was the need to find some top quality horses. Clint confided in Sr. Bond that he was breeding the best line of horses that he could. Clint had some superior horses by now, but would like to buy two or three additional top quality mares or stallions. Sr. Bond had seen some of Clint's horses and confessed that his ranch stock did not reach the quality of Clint's existing stock. However, he had heard that a large land grant holder south of Albuquerque, who was at least one day's ride away, had brought such horses over from Europe years ago.

This ranch he spoke of was one of the original Spanish land grants given to a Spanish nobleman by the name of Perez. It was Sr. Bond's understanding that this family still owned a lot of the original land grant. The horses were brought as gifts from the royal family in Spain as a payment for the Perez family's contributions in settling the New Mexico Territory for Spain. The story was that these horses could out-run the other western horses. They were bred for strength and endurance. Sr. Bond had been at a horse race near Santa Fe several years ago when two of the Perez horses took every race. Those horses were so fast that after a few races none of the other horse owners would let their horses compete against them.

The word was that the Perez Ranch did not sell their horses because they wanted to keep this high quality horse line for themselves. But, the rumor also had it that some of the Indian tribes south of the Perez ranch had stolen some of the horses in the past. They in time had also developed some pretty good horses. Clint's best chance of getting his hands on that breeding line might be through the southern Apache tribe. That particular tribe was difficult to deal with, but they did often run out of food during each winter. A small herd of sheep might do the trick for a trade for a few top quality horses. Sr. Bond told Clint that each winter a group of Spanish land grant holders would meet in Albuquerque to exchange information about politics and any pending threats to their grant holdings. This organization of those of Spanish ancestry had a paid, long-supported lobbyist in the U.S. capital and Mexico City to represent their interests. The next meeting was scheduled just before New Year's Day. The Perez ranch usually had a representative at the meeting. So, Sr. Bond would inquire about the possibility that Clint could buy some horses directly from the Perez Ranch.

The last item was the trading for the sawmill work, lumber and logs. Sr. Bond had seen some of the Pecos blankets at the Santa Fe market square and had decided that he would like payment in blankets. His main ranch house could use a number of them for floor coverings and wall decorations. So, it was agreed that at the November meeting in the Santa Fe Western Plaza Hotel, Clint would bring a selection of Pecos blankets for Sr. Bond to pick through. In response, Sr. Bond would send four more wagon loads of lumber and roof posts to Rio Pecos immediately. He wanted plenty of established credit so he could pick a choice selection of blankets.

Clint headed back to Santa Fe for a few days of entertainment and the opportunity to make some money the fun way – gambling.

It took a good day to clean up his house and barn. Not the kind of pleasure he had come for, but it had to be done. A trip to the feed store and all the barn stalls were well stocked for a few months. Then he dressed down to his Mexican hide-trader look and hit the gaming tables. It must have been payday for the soldiers for they were throwing around shiny $20 gold pieces. The word around town was they had not been paid for six months. The payroll wagon in the late spring had been robbed by bandits up around the Raton Pass. The new payroll wagon had just arrived with a heavy guard unit. That explained why extra men were being sent to Santa Fe command to start building Fort Union.

The other piece of information from back east told of a political split between the northern and the southern states. So, these additional soldiers were being sent to defend the New Mexico Territory's capital of Santa Fe if war broke out. It was rumored that a group of people in Texas had organized an army and might try to take Santa Fe if fighting broke out back east.

Clint was busy making some easy money from the hard drinking but reckless soldiers. He kept his winnings at a moderate level at each table and moved around between gambling houses over a two-day spree. He pulled in enough gold coins that he had to make three trips to his hideaway house in order to unload.

During Clint's last day in Santa Fe before heading back to Rio Pecos, he made a hefty deposit of gold coins into his bank account. Mr. Jenson was always glad to receive these deposits. His bank was funding several builders in the region, thus he could use all the capital that his bank could attract.

Mr. Jenson had heard that Clint had purchased a rundown house on the lower side of town. If Clint was interested in more of those old houses, he knew several that the owners were desperate to cash out. In fact, the house right beside the one he had purchased was being foreclosed on by this bank. If Clint would pay the balance on a discounted loan which was less than $200, the bank would turn the building and lot over to Clint. The bank didn't want to own and maintain any property. The house was in terrible shape, but the three-stall barn and lot space would be great for stabling horses. Clint knew the house and he agreed to the purchase. He had made many times over that much money in two days at the gambling tables. This double house, barn stalls and open lot would make an excellent station when he traveled, and also for storage. Clint spent a few hours with Mr. Jenson signing all the papers and seeing them recorded before he headed back to Rio Pecos.

When he pulled onto the little plateau overlooking Rio Pecos Compound, he was impressed with its progress. The new adobe buildings and the new footers were forming a mall area with the original adobe ranch house at one end and a water well building and community workshops at the other. In addition, all along the mall were new adobe buildings and even a few frame houses. The general store and trading post were arranged along one side as well as along the building that housed the school.

The Kansas carpenters had built several covered boardwalks in front of some of the buildings. He could see that the large stable and blacksmith shop had new living quarters attached along one side. Clint was impressed with the progress and the workers he could see were hard at the task. Clint could see six or maybe seven new foundations where some adobe block was being laid.

Clint's method of making sure the materials were available, provide a general plan, then getting out of the way was producing unbelievable results. He wondered if the compound people realized how much they had created out of mud and lumber.

The new adobe buildings were almost identical to the style and workmanship of the original ranch house. Thus, Clint was sure that Juan Cruz's ancestors had probably help build the ranch house.

Several people observed Clint's return, so it wasn't long before a group had gathered in front of his home. Juan Cruz said his group was ready to bring the rest of his clan to Rio Pecos if he could get some wagons, horses and guards. The Navajos had made quite a bit of jewelry out of the new gems and would like to make a trading trip to the market square. They too would like some protection for their trip. The Kansas school teachers would like to obtain more school supplies if Clint would fund such an expenditure. Finally, the head Mexican guard would like to escort the whole wagon train to Santa Fe and San Juan Pueblo with all his men. If he could give them some leave time in Santa Fe, they would really appreciate the break. The Basque group just wanted some basic supplies, but didn't want to make the trip. They would stay at the compound to provide cover while everyone was away. The Basques knew that the Navajos and Pueblos were better traders than they were, so they were welcome to trade the Basques' wool for their needed supplies.

Listening to all those plans, Clint could see that this community had worked everything out between themselves. All he had to do was to stay out of the way . . . and nothing would please him more.

The group was told about the two houses and the barns purchased in Santa Fe that were in need of major repairs. Clint's plan was to have some of the men take turns working on these two houses and barns while they were in Santa Fe. The barns could store their trade stuff and would be a lot closer to the market square. Some of the traders could stay in the second house and keep watch on their supplies. Most everyone would still have to camp out at the traders' campsite south of town. The in-town buildings would be a convenient storage and resting place for the traders during the day.

Within the week, the caravan was headed to Santa Fe. The Pueblo men were riding some of

Clint's freshly broken horses, so it could be a rough trip for them. Joe Black was sending three new wagons on this trip along with all the old wagons in top shape. The blacksmith was proud of his handiwork, but was staying behind. Santa Fe had not been kind to him in the past. He now had a comfortable new place, and people that appreciated his craft. Rio Pecos was his home.

On arriving at Santa Fe, most of the wagons were unloaded into the barn and house that Clint had just purchased. The three new wagons plus Juan Cruz's wagons were sent out empty to San Juan Pueblo. Some of the Pueblo and Navajo women set up their trading stations at the market square. The Kansas carpenters and two of Juan's men started repairing the run-down house and barn. The balance of wagons and tents were set up out at the traders' camp.

Clint knew they were going to be stretched rather thin for protection. Three guards had gone with Juan to help move the Cruz clan to Rio Pecos. Given the two locations in Santa Fe, plus the market place, providing adequate protection was very difficult. Clint spent most of his time behind the scenes trying to spot any trouble that might be brewing.

Having the reputation that harm would quickly come to anyone who messed with Rio Pecos and its people probably helped, but there was always that risk that the spoils looked too good and a raid might be tried. Clint was spending most of his surveillance time watching over the pottery and jewelry traders. These trades were mostly in cash and a lot of money was changing hands. Besides, the jewelry was easy to carry and hide if stolen.

Clint was also aware that most people wouldn't associate the Pueblo and Navajo traders with the Rio Pecos Compound. Thus the reputation of that association may not work as well as planned.

Clint's guess about the particular target that a robber might choose was right. The sudden attack came when two of the pueblo women along with one of the Kansas carpenters were walking from the market square back to the old house with a load of cash. The attack came quickly. Four men surrounded them, knocked them down and stripped them of all their bags. Clint was too far away to stop the beating, but he did get a good look at all four men and their horses. When he got to the fallen people, they were hurt, but not seriously. One woman had a big gash in the back of her head and it was bleeding. Clint went to the house for help. Once they were settled into a safe place, it was time for payback.

It didn't take long for Clint to spot the horses at one of the saloon hitching rails across town. He slipped up and cut the saddle cinch on each horse so they could not ride off. Then he moved into the saloon to see what he was up against. The four men had joined two others at a table near the back door. They were enjoying the fruits of their evil deeds. Clint got a drink and moved close enough to hear part of the conversation. They were discussing the way they would spend their easy money. The top floor of this saloon had a lot of beautiful women that would entertain you for a fee, and they had enough money between them to stay for a day or two. It was agreed that two of them would walk all six horses down the block to the saloon's stable, then rejoin their friends upstairs.

Clint eased himself out the saloon doors and worked his way down to the stable. As a serve yourself, this stable had no attendant. Clint was beginning to think the robbers might have changed their plans. It was almost an hour before the six horses were brought in and stalled. The two men were so intent on their task of retrieving some cash and jewelry out of their saddlebags that the first one dropped with a single blow on the head. The second was drawing his gun when Clint's club put out his lights. The whole thing was over in a split-second, and all was quiet again. Clint then went through everything and collected the loot these two had with them.

Some of the jewelry was not the Rio Pecos type so it was probably taken from other traders. Clint wrapped the two bodies in canvas sheets and loaded them on their horses. He then mounted one of the horses that did not have the cinch cut and led all the other five out the back alley and out of town. He located a wash that was not too far off a well-traveled path. The two bodies were laid out, and then Clint cut their throats for effect. The horses were stripped and turned loose. Clint rode one horse bareback close to the saloon and then turned it loose. He had recovered almost the complete amount that had been taken from his people. He also knew who the remaining four were and would deal with them later. Now it was time to check on the health of his friends.

A lot of pain was lessened when they saw that most of their money and jewelry was recovered. No questions were asked as to how Clint had gotten their money, as he then headed back to the saloon and boarding house to see what the remaining four thieves were up to. To Clint's surprise there was a lot of excitement about a shootout. It seemed that the four men had gone upstairs for a while, then one of them came down and went to the stable up the street. Shortly thereafter, word came back that they had been robbed by some of their own people. A big fight broke out near the stable and two of the four were shot. The sheriff had taken the other two to jail and would try to sort out their stories. One surviving shooter accused the other men of stealing his horse and money. The other survivor contended that someone else had stolen their horses and must have taken their two friends hostage. Clint listened for a while to the numerous possibilities that were flying around the saloon. Most of the customers thought that these six were all crooks and had gotten into a fight over money or women. No one seemed to care a lot.

To most of the people in the saloon, including the deputy sheriff, this was a fight among thieves. Business as usual would be the order of the day. Clint felt that his revenge was adequate. When the other bodies would be discovered, it would only add to the mystery and to the legend of a protective dark angel around Rio Pecos people. He would try to encourage that myth in a few comments here and there. A good myth or tale was so much easier to remember than any bits of the truth.

The next day saw the Cruz clan and all their wagons and cattle arrive at the traders' camp. It was agreed to stay for a few days while all the trading was completed and everyone had had a chance to shop and relax in Santa Fe. The relaxing was mostly for the young people and especially some of the young Mexican guards. But this arrangement only lasted one day, because the Cruz family wanted to head out toward Rio Pecos. They had cattle and horses to herd and the families wanted to get to their new homes. Juan knew he had a lot of building to complete before winter weather arrived. Two of the guards had had enough of spending their money and agreed to go with the Cruz clan.

The Kansas carpenters said they needed at least four more days to finish the repairs on the old Santa Fe house and barn. They had moved into the building while the repairs were underway. This put them close to the market square so they could keep watch over the goods and supplies of the Pueblos and Navajos.

The Rio Pecos people were having very little trouble from the riff-raff and the thieves. The two bodies had been found out at the edge of town in an arroyo wash with their throats cut. The legend of a vigilant or dark angel protecting the Rio Pecos traders was circulating around the square and beyond.

The sheriff's men and even the U.S. Marshal had come by to question the Rio Pecos Compound people as to what they knew about the killings.

The guards convinced Clint to stay in Santa Fe through the weekend. Then the entire caravan headed out to Rio Pecos. They were well-stocked for the coming bad weather and to complete the last of the houses for the Cruz families. The bigger buildings would be build next spring and summer. Some of the rock footers could be done during any weather breaks during the winter. Winters were fairly mild there with the exception of an occasional storm, but that never lasted more than a week or so.

The trip back to the compound was made especially enjoyable because of the successful results from the pottery and jewelry sales. The new clay had done wonders for the pottery makers. They had sold nearly everything at a good price. The new stones had been used in only a few pieces of jewelry which had sold at a little better than average price, but then the colors were new to a lot of the shoppers.

Chapter 15

Rio Pecos Compound was gradually developing into an active little village. Clint was busy just keeping materials available to the builders. The blanket-weaving needed for the trade with Sr. Bond was almost complete. A meeting was scheduled for the upcoming November weekend at the Western Plaza Hotel.

The drivers from the Bond Ranch should have the needed information about the Apache territory. The Navajos were already making plans to return to their homeland come spring or early summer. Clint just hoped that it would be safe enough for them to make the trip.

The meeting to discuss the sheep drive at the Western Plaza Hotel presented Clint with some real surprises. The sheep owner who was north of Las Vegas, Sr. Manuel Ortega, brought up the names of Atkinson and Johnson as the reasons he had gotten out of the sheep business. His land had been split by a new survey done by Atkinson for a firm out of St. Louis. A firm with a partner named Claude Johnson from Española.

The land title work had been done by a lawyer from St. Louis with both Atkinson and Johnson testifying at the land title hearing. The judge had ruled that Sr. Ortega's land grant was about one-half of what his original grant had provided. So he had lost some of his best grazing land and water rights. In addition to these legal problems with his land titles, the raids against his herds were continuing. Several of his shepherds had been killed and now the rest were afraid to tend the sheep. He was going to have to get rid of all his sheep with this one last drive. He had doubts that his men would ever help. They were so afraid for their lives and for their sheep. If Sr. Bond would bring more guards and maybe another shepherd, he might be able to persuade his men to make the final drive to Kansas.

Clint then heard a story about a dozen of these Atkinson gunmen being left on foot down on the Santa Fe Trail south of Las Vegas. The bandits had been robbed of everything including their horses and pack mules. Clint used his well-trained poker face so that he did not display any of the smiles he felt inside.

The story included a big ruckus that had happened when these dozen or so men walked back into Las Vegas and faced up to the raging Atkinson. His men had been bushwhacked and outwitted and they were mad and mean over the next few weeks, causing numerous fights and shootings as they went about reestablishing their reputations as top guns.

Clint felt sorry for the harm that had come Sr. Ortega's way. His problems had started long before Clint had bushwhacked Atkinson's men, but the cruelty had intensified after Clint's handiwork. Besides, Clint had no idea that the men that had been planning a raid against his people were associated with neither Atkinson nor the illegal claims against Rio Pecos Ranch.

This armed and organized Atkinson crew was a real problem for Clint's planned drive north. The safety of his men and Ortega's people would be at risk if they joined the drive. Clint knew he had spooked Johnson. Maybe a little extra pressure just before the drive could divert the Atkinson gang's attention and keep them away from the sheep drive.

Clint could see a pattern with Atkinson's land purchases. Most of the land was top grazing land with good water. The sheep herds were not stolen, but scattered or killed. The sheep ranching business was being seriously disrupted or driven out. This looked like the same process that had been used in Texas to replace sheep ranching with cattle. Clint felt sure that there was somehow a connection with the cattle business.

It was also becoming clear that all these problems led back to St. Louis. Ortega was convinced that Atkinson was behind all of this, but had no proof. The Ortega family had owned the land grant for over 100 years without any claims against it until this new Atkinson survey had been presented.

Part of the meeting was the selecting of blankets by both Ortega and Bond. It soon became obvious that Ortega was not lacking funds. He selected and paid in gold for some of the best Rio Pecos blankets. Sr. Bond was satisfied with his trade of lumber and logs. The two Navajos who were with Clint carried the balance of blankets to their wagon outside. These blankets needed to be taken back to the market square and put on display. The Rio Pecos people were having some great trading days.

Bond, Ortega and Clint had agreed to start the drive from Española and Rio Pecos on the night of the last full moon in May. Ortega would try to have his men and sheep ready two weeks later to join Clint's herd. If the Ortega men were not willing to go on the drive, then Clint agreed to add the Ortega sheep to his drive at three cents per head. Everyone agreed they could get three times that amount if delivered to the Abilene, Kansas, rail head.

Sr. Bond then reported on the Apache territory. The U.S. Government had sent more troops to the Durango area to protect the miners and government surveyors. They had succeeded in reducing the raids against the settlers and had partially confined the Apaches to an area due south of Durango in the New Mexico Territory.

If you traveled north through the Raton Pass, then turned due west along the trail to Durango, you would miss the area where the Apache were being contained. The government was not providing sufficient protection for the Hopi and Navajo tribes, so some raiding continued among these three Indian tribes. Apache raiding parties were also still hitting wagon trains and sheep and cattle herds down along the Choma River south of the Apache area. The Apache had even carried out some raids down on the Rio Grande against some of the northern Pueblo villages. Sr. Bond was aware of these raids. In fact, his men had helped to drive the Apache range warriors back north. Sr. Bond painted a somewhat mixed picture of the Apache conditions the Navajos would face if they tried to return to their homeland.

Sr. Bond thought that the Ute Indians may prove to be a bigger problem for the Navajos as they went from Durango southwest to their homeland. Two Ute tribes were being squeezed by the westward movement of settlers. The mining around Durango had driven the Utes out of their good hunting areas, so they were fighting back with some vicious raids against anyone they could find. This included the miners, settlers, ranchers and even other Indian tribes.

Clint then learned from Sr. Ortega that he was headed to the Perez Ranch and Albuquerque for a month. He would be there for the New Year's meeting with the Spanish land grant holders. Sr. Ortega often spent the winter in Albuquerque with its warmer climate, home to many Spanish people. It was time to socialize and tell their old stories of their ancestors. The influence of the Mexican culture was taking over many of their customs, but Ortega's group was doing what they could to preserve their heritage in this wild and lawless land.

Clint offered to send two or three of his best mares with Ortega to the Perez Ranch. This would give the Perez family a chance to look at the quality of the horses that Clint had developed so far. If they would agree to breed his mares, he would retrieve them come summer. Ortega had seen some of Clint's horses and he felt that Clint had already developed a breed line almost as good as the Perez horses. He would be glad and proud to present Clint's breeding option to the Perez family.

Clint's help on the sheep drive north was greatly appreciated, so Ortega would be more than willing to help pay back the favor by working with the Perez family on Clint's horse deal.

The return trip to Rio Pecos gave Clint plenty of time to go over the risks and possible options with some of the Navajos. He could tell that the Navajos were set on returning to their homeland. However, it was also revealed that two or three of the Navajo people wanted to stay on at Rio Pecos Ranch. It seems that two of the young Navajo girls had made friends with two young men from the ranch. One of the Pueblo boys and one of the Mexican guards had already asked the Navajo leader for permission to court the girls. The Navajo leader was not happy about the arrangement, but knew he faced many risks of getting these young ladies back to Navajo land. Besides, the security and living conditions at Rio Pecos were getting better all the time. So he had reluctantly agreed for the young women to see their young men. Juan Cruz was just as opposed to one of his Pueblo girls dating a Navajo, but he also was persuaded by the girl to give his blessing. The two Navajo young women were among the best new talents in blanket-weaving that the community had produced. They had been very receptive to incorporating some of the Basque dyes and wool into the Navajo blanket patterns. Their blankets were getting the highest prices on the market square.

The third Navajo that wanted to stay at Rio Pecos was a young man who made Navajo silver and turquoise jewelry. He had developed some excellent skills in using the new turquoise stone from the nearby mountains. His jewelry had also been well received at the Santa Fe trading square.

William F. Martin

He wanted to continue his craft here and in Santa
Fe. The desire to return to the old ways and
hardships of his family's homeland did not seem
attractive to him. His youth and energies were
drawing him more toward Santa Fe. The good
life and protection of the Rio Pecos Compound
allowed him to concentrate on his art of jewelry
making.

Chapter 16

The winter months passed rapidly. The spring lambing was almost over with a bumper crop. The organizing for the May drive to Kansas would need to start in two months. The sheep herds had to be culled, separated and marked. Those sheep being selected for the drive were then moved to the northern-most grazing area on the ranch.

Most of the Navajos had decided to move north in spite of the dangers and hardships they may face. One older Navajo lady and her immediate family were going to stay at Rio Pecos. The young lady that was marrying the Pueblo man was her daughter and the other young woman that was marrying the Mexican guard was her sister's daughter. This older lady had three other children and they too were all staying. Her man had left them long before they had moved to Rio Pecos. Her sheep herd was doing well on the Rio Pecos range, besides her blankets and wool were bringing good prices in Santa Fe. And that market was less than a two-day ride from her home. Up north, she had had trips that took over a week just to get to the nearest trading post. Also the grazing on the Rio Pecos was more than twice as good as her old family home area. While she did miss some of the old ways, she did not miss the extreme hardships. Her children were going to school with the Kansas settlers and were learning a lot. All of them could now read and write some English and that was helping a lot at the Santa Fe market square. In fact, her children were becoming better traders than she ever was. The new method of blanket weaving that her daughter and niece had done was the best among all for sale on the Santa Fe square.

The Mexican guards had just about wiped out the threats of coyote and cougar to her sheep. The harassment that she and her people used to face had almost disappeared. She knew that several gunmen had been killed that had given the Rio Pecos people trouble. That disappearance and murder of several bad men last fall in Santa Fe had just about been the end of troubles for her people. Problems now were either drunks or young men flirting with the very pretty young Navajo and Pueblo girls. Such problems were old ones and she knew how to handle them.

Juan Cruz and family were back laying adobe brick for the new buildings. The winter had been mild, so that many of the stone footers had been completed before spring. Collecting and hauling the rocks for the footers and foundations did take a lot more effort and time than the first few buildings had. The rocks that were close and easy to gather had been used. They now were having to spread out more and more to get a load of suitable rocks. All of the Cruz clan was finally housed in permanent homes. There was still a lot of work to do on them, but even in their current condition, they were a lot better off than their old homes in San Juan Pueblo and Juan was very pleased with the quality of the adobe. The clay pits on the Rio Pecos Ranch were producing the best material that he had ever worked with, and his people were making more money off the new clay pottery than they had ever made. He was still upset that his son wanted to marry a Navajo girl, even though she was from a good hard-working family and her blanket-weaving skills were the best that Juan had seen. Juan was already in trouble with his tribal council because of an earlier cross-tribe marriage. However, that couple seemed to be making a good life for themselves here at Rio Pecos. Juan was going to take a wagonload of top quality potter clay to the San Juan Pueblo, hoping this gesture would soften any hard feelings the old villagers were having toward his family.

Juan was hoping that the passage of two or three years would heal the rift between his clan and the other tribal leaders. He did miss the community celebrations, big community feasts, and tribal fellowship and support. He had uneasy feelings of being out of his place and away from his roots. It was hard to explain to himself because he enjoyed the work of building a new village. His people were safe and doing better than they ever had before. Maybe time would lessen these vague feelings of being out of place or of losing a little of yourself.

The Basque clan was ready for the long drive to Kansas. It was their hope to find some top quality rams during this drive. They were not pleased with the crossbreeding that Clint was encouraging. It was true the new crossbreed was tougher and endured this region better, but the wool was not as good as their original breed line. The flavor of the crossbred mutton was also better than their pure Merino sheep. However, the

Basque were skilled at raising sheep and were convinced they could develop a breed line with all the qualities they wanted. Their carts and wagons were in top shape and everyone was ready for the new adventure.

The Kansas settlers were very happy to stay at the ranch. They still remembered their tragic trip from Kansas to Rio Pecos and had no interest in doing that again. The settlers had finally made peace with themselves and accepted their new location as their home. The school teaching and carpentry work had everyone busy. These settlers had produced a good garden last year and were preparing for an even better one this year. The Indians had given them seeds and several good tips on growing chilies and beans in this climate. Clint had even found them a few milk cows and a bull.

Two guards had agreed to stay behind and help out around the compound. The horse herd was their responsibility although most of the horses would be used on the drive. Both guards had girlfriends and wanted to stay close anyway. The guards had worked with Joe Black to train most of the people to keep their weapons clean and ready for use. Clint had obtained some of the best rifles and pistols available at this time. Crooks and bandits always seemed to have the best guns. Somehow those weapons were finding their way to Rio Pecos Compound. Joe Black always seemed to have a steady supply of new guns even though he never left Rio Pecos. Further, Joe's gunsmithing skills made him fairly good at updating and repairing all types of guns.

The Juan Cruz clan organized a big feast and dance for the sheep drive sendoff. The whole community came together and shared their favorite dishes in a display suitable for a king or Indian chief. It was so much fun for everyone that there was talk of making it an annual affair. Although there was also some sadness because a lot of families would be separated for three or four months, most of the young people that were making the drive were excited and ready to get started. They did not have the fear of the unknown that their parents held.

Early the next morning the drive started up the Santa Fe Trail. The wagons, carts and horses took the main trail heading to the first main campsite. The sheep were moved along at a steady pace, just fast enough to make time, but slow enough to keep their weight on them.

Clint, along with Joe Black and two of the Mexican guards, would stay behind to protect Rio Pecos, and most of the Pueblo men and Kansas men headed out on a separate mission. This group plus the wagons, spare horses, and carts made up a sizable caravan. Clint made sure that everyone was heavily armed with a maximum display of the latest weaponry. The most striking thing about this group of people was their dress code. Every man and boy was wearing dark clothing that looked like a uniform. The caravan looked like an army or heavily armed guard unit. Clint led this group straight up the Santa Fe Trail to Las Vegas. By midmorning the next day, Clint, in his most military manner, presented a set of surveys to the land office clerk. The entire parade of uniformed men was standing in the street in front of the land title office as Clint presented his made-up, but official-looking survey documents. Clint demanded that the hearing notice for his title challenge of Atkinson's surveys of the Ortega land grant be posted immediately. Then, with three of his armed body guards, he left the office and led the military-looking unit out of town headed north. As soon as they came to a good hiding place, all the uniforms were stripped off, wagons' special covers removed, and everything put on pack horses. Then, all the men that were not making the drive to Kansas headed back to Rio Pecos with the uniforms. They broke up into small groups and stayed off the main trail. The wagons, carts and horses for the drive moved off the main trail to a predetermined campsite to await the sheep herd.

So far everyone was carrying out their assigned tasks with precision. Clint then went on spy duty to watch for Atkinson and his gunmen. It was only a few hours after Clint's visit to the land office that Atkinson and a dozen armed riders pulled up at the land office front hitching rail. Clint watched with his spyglass as the title clerk came out onto the boardwalk and pointed north as he talked to Atkinson. The Atkinson men broke into three groups and headed out both north and south with one group waiting for Atkinson at the land title office hitching rail. It was late evening before all the Atkinson riders had returned to Las Vegas to report. Clint switched to being the Mexican hide-trader and went to one of the café saloons nearest Atkinson's big fancy hotel. Rumors were flying about the double claim against the Ortega land grant. This new challenge to Atkinson's claim on the Ortega Ranch had the old man in an uproar. The word was out that Atkinson had sent for Claude Johnson to join him here in the Las Vegas hotel as soon as possible. It also looked as though all of Atkinson's gunmen had been called into Las Vegas. This was what Clint had been hoping for. With Atkinson's attention on protecting his illegal claims, it would allow time for the Rio Pecos sheep herds to meet up with the Ortega herd and get north through the Raton Pass.

Clint then headed to the Ortega Ranch to alert them of the possible hornet's nest that had been disturbed. He was not surprised to see a well-fortified Ortega main complex. Their sheep herds had been raided while scattered over the range. Some of the herds had been killed. However, there had never been any attacks against the main ranch complex and Clint could see why.

The Ortega herd was already on the move to the Raton Pass when Clint reached the ranch house. The Ortega herders had decided to make the drive when they learned of the extra money to be made and the armed guards that would be making the trip. Sr. Ortega had also given them some hope of joining the Rio Pecos Ranch after the drive. With the loss of the Navajo herders, Clint's ranch might just be short of manpower. Clint confirmed Sr. Ortega's idea about the need for more sheep men after the drive. He would offer them the same arrangement that was working well for his Basque families. Sr. Ortega was closing down the sheep ranching activities at his ranch.

The information received about the Albuquerque land grant holders meeting was troublesome. Sr. Perez had told Sr. Ortega that his east coast contacts felt that one of the big eastern families was funding the railroad system's purchasing of western lands. The money was being funneled through an agency in St. Louis. Both Atkinson and Johnson were shareholders in that St. Louis operation. As far as the records were available to inspect, they indicated the St. Louis agency as a real estate firm. The firm had been set up to acquire lands along the proposed railroad right-of-ways. The only possible illegal activity that Sr. Perez's contacts had uncovered was the possible conflict of interest between Atkinson's surveyor role and his partial ownership in the real estate firm. It did appear that a lot of property along the proposed railroad route had been obtained by Johnson and Atkinson even before the surveyed routes had been made public.

It then appeared that a lot of the land purchased by the St. Louis office was coming from Atkinson and Johnson at surprisingly good prices. These costs were then being passed on to the railroad companies in addition to extra profits to the St. Louis agency, in which Atkinson was a shareholder.

Sr. Ortega had asked the lobbyist to make inquiries into this whole railroad right-of-way acquisition process with an especially close look at Atkinson's surveyor role.

The word about Claude Johnson was that his family had ties to some of the railroad owners and the eastern financing sources. He had married into big money; however his wife never wanted to travel or leave the east coast family.

When Claude's father-in-law had died a few years ago, the estate management was turned over to Claude. That started Claude's rapid development of a western ranch near Española and the acquisition of large tracts of land. As far as Perez and Ortega's contacts could tell, Claude's wife had almost disappeared from public life after her father's death. It was suspected that Claude was rapidly running through the family's wealth. With this new information, Clint was armed with plenty to follow-up on when the drive was completed.

The other great piece of information that Sr. Ortega brought back from Sr. Perez and the Albuquerque meeting was that Clint's mares would be bred with the Spanish horses. Clint could arrange to retrieve his mares immediately after the Kansas drive.

Chapter 17

Don Perea had heard of a place just east of Santa Fe, New Mexico, that could solve a major life and death problem for him. The sheep rancher he had worked for over the past 20 years had been killed by bandits. The raid had also killed his wife, one of his sons, a brother and his three children. His one son, a brother and sister-in-law were all that were left of the family. A major portion of the sheep herd had been scattered or stolen. Perea's life savings had been tied to that herd. He had developed a ten percent ownership over the years, plus his house was also destroyed along with the owner's ranch house and barns. Although he did not know the bandits, it was rumored that they were Texans supported by a major cattle firm that wanted to move into the area.

What was left of his meager belongings, along with his family, had been hiding out in the foothills through the winter. But now the cottonwoods along the river beds were turning green and yellow. Though it had frosted three or four times over the past two weeks, the main winter weather was over. Their supplies were running out and he had been able to obtain only a few food basics from wagons down on the old trail leading into Santa Fe. It was during one of these trading trips that a cousin of his had shared with him the rumor of a safe place. His cousin was working for another major sheep rancher further north. That rancher had fortified his ranch holdings and hired some Mexican ex-soldiers to protect them. However, some raids had reduced his flocks and the cost of hiring protection was causing some real concern. At the moment, Perea's cousin, along with another 20 men, several wagons and armed guards were taking meat and wool to Santa Fe to sell and trade for supplies. His cousin's last trip to Santa Fe, about six months ago, had also turned up the rumor about a compound on the Pecos River that gave protection to hard-working families if they agreed to join and participate in ranching for the owner.

He had also overheard a discussion between two hard cases, apparent thieves, outside a saloon. They were relating a story about a gang that had raided one of the sheep herds near this compound. The eight rustlers had lost nine men before they could get out of the valley without a single head of sheep. Then, within a week, two of the remaining four bandits had been assassinated with no clue as to who was protecting these herds and the people.

The word was also out that one of the most vicious gangs in the territory had robbed a supply train going to this Rio Pecos Compound. The gang leader disappeared about a week later. His gun belt was left hanging on the trail entrance to the compound. Then, over the next few days, several of the gang members were also mysteriously killed without anyone taking credit. The balance of the gang left Santa Fe without a trace.

And one more story was about a young woman from the compound. She had been harassed and beaten during a shopping trip into Santa Fe. Several of the supply train workers that had accompanied her had also beaten and robbed. Apparently the local law was not very protective of the herd's people.

Bands of ex-soldiers, gunmen, rustlers and unemployed miners roamed the streets of Santa Fe at will, taking what they wanted. The meanest and toughest got the goods, and everyone else just bowed their heads and tried not to get involved. The three roughnecks that had harassed the compound people had made no secret of that fact, even bragging of how easy it was to fleece a herder and their women. Soon all three men were found with their throats cut, the loot missing, and their gun belts hanging on a trail post east of Santa Fe.

Thus, the word was out far and wide to leave the Rio Pecos Compound people alone. The ruthless deaths of gunmen that had violated these compound people's rights had developed into a real deterrent for would-be troublemakers. Actually, the secret killing of the toughest of the outlaws was the most unnerving.

Don Perea was at his wits' end, so why not take the risk to seek out the Rio Pecos hiding place? At this point, he had little to lose. The winter had left them broke and without food. They might starve to death in the makeshift shelter up against the cliffs. Besides, with spring in the air, the bandit raids might start again. Don Perea had only one brother, one son and a widowed sister-in-law for family. Only four of his herdsmen had survived and the meager flock they had rounded up was kept scattered in the hills. It would only be a matter of time before the bandits found this small herd and its keepers.

His cousin was not sure of the exact Rio Pecos Compound location. The most likely location was due east of Santa Fe through the Gloriata Pass to the Pecos River. He would guess that a northerly path following the river should bring you to the area. Don Perea's current location was well north and on the Canadian River Basin. If he could take the Santa Fe Trail south, cross over the divide between the Canadian and Pecos Rivers, then follow the Pecos River south, his path should lead him across the lands of the rumored safe compound.

If the people guarding this compound were as ruthless as his cousin believed, then he might be killed on site. However, staying put was almost certain death. At least a searching trip, no matter how dangerous, would be doing something. He asked his brother, his son, and two herdsmen to stay with his sister-in-law. Don would take two herders and a very small herd of sheep south to find the new place. Their cover would be simple sheep herders moving their sheep further south to warmer range, typical for sheep ranching. The small number and the rag-tag look of sheep and herders would not make it worth the trouble for bandits. The real risk would be roaming gunmen, unemployed miners and gangs of thugs that could harass them for pure meanness at little risk of harm to themselves.

The path south would be off the trail through fairly thick underbrush. This would hopefully discourage most of those lazy gangs that robbed rather than worked. The sheep were very accustomed to foraging the rough slopes and underbrush. In fact, the grazing along the riverbed was great for the sheep. They would probably put on several pounds during the trip.

Just before beginning the trip, his brother and sister-in-law suggested that Don take as many sheep as he could to reduce the chances that bandits would find the larger herd if left behind. So, the new plan was for him to take about 400 herd of sheep south. That would leave less than 50 sheep for his brother to manage. This much smaller number could be scattered out and hidden much easier.

The march south was slow, but not difficult. The mountain ridge between the Canadian and Pecos Rivers was little more than an elevated plateau. The grass was lush compared to their hiding place for the last two months. Moving across the open grass plain was risky, but the only path to the Rio Pecos headwaters. When they crossed the main trail to Santa Fe, they would be at their most critical exposure. The herd was spread out and taken across in small groups. And every one dragged brush behind themselves to reduce and mask the tracks as much as possible.

They were less than half a mile off the trail when a small band of riders came along the main trail. The riders milled around the crossing for a while. Don Perea could see that a discussion was going on among the riders. It included a lot of pointing first up the trail and then south toward Don's path.

Apparently, the group decided it wasn't worth further investigation because they continued the northern direction. Don was sure the decision to break the herd into small groups worked and had discouraged the riders. It didn't appear worth their time and effort. They could see the heavy underbrush where the sheep trail was leading. Most horse riders tried to avoid these tangles of heavy growth. The brush on this semi-arid terrain was tough and thorny. It could tear a horse up rather quickly. Sheep on the other hand seemed to thrive in this cover. The brush provided shade for grass to grow under it and the sheep being small, wooly and agile could graze around and under the thorny growth. Even the bush itself was food, especially the new growth.

This Curry sheep strain that made up his herd was especially adapted to survival on rough range and limited food and water and they had the best tasting meat. These little long-haired, wooly creatures were the ugliest of the many sheep strains, but most suited to this New Mexico Territory terrain. Even though most sheep ranchers in Spain and the eastern part of America preferred the Murino sheep for its fine wool and plumper body, the Murino was no match for the Curry in this mountainous region with its limited rainfall and scarce vegetation. Besides, the Indian tribes up north had developed a good wool blanket trade using the long, coarse wool of the Curry. So the Churro produced a special type of wool for this region, and was valued for its wool, plus its high-quality mutton.

Don Perea and his herdsmen worked their way down the mostly dry bed of the Pecos River. There was enough river flow that pools of water were abundant. The hard river bed made traveling a lot easier than the thick brush along the river banks. Over a week had passed since they had crossed the old Santa Fe Trail. Their herd had grown in numbers as stray sheep joined the flock. It appeared that several herds had been scattered here over time, but many of the newcomers were in poor health due to cuts, sore hoofs, and even a few gunshots. Don's crew was well experienced in tending sheep. All but two of the 30-some strays they collected were saved. Those two with gunshots were slaughtered for meat and wool.

The drive south was deliberately slow. Don did not want to seem aggressive or to have any particular destination in mind. If he could present himself as a lowly herder just following the grass south, he may pull this off. The major uncertainty surrounded his destination and the question, did this safe compound really exist or was it only a rumor? If they didn't come on the Rio Pecos Compound soon, he must turn back or return to fetch the rest of the herd. This area was definitely better to winter the sheep than where they had been hiding out up north. The foliage was much better and the drop in elevation was increasing the temperature as well as reducing the wind exposure.

The discussion around the campfire that night resulted in a plan of action. They would continue for two more days on this southerly path. If they had not contacted any of the compound people by then, two of the herders would stay with the sheep and continue slowly moving south. Don and the youngest herders would head back north and bring the family and remaining herd south to join them. The two pack horses they had left with the widowed sister-in-law, one son, and his one surviving brother, would be brought down. If they ran into trouble, the horses would be abandoned and they would retreat south down the same path along the river bed.

Late the following day, as evening camp was being set up, one of the herdsmen reported hearing the tinkle of a bell. It could be the sound of a sheep bell that a lot of shepherds used to track their herds. Don climbed onto the highest point, trying to spot any signs of other campfires. Nothing could be seen, but again he heard the faint sound of a bell. As the sun was coming up, Don and one helper were well on their way, pushing south along the Pecos River toward that bell sound.

It was almost midmorning when they came upon the first small group of sheep grazing near the river bank. These sheep were well fed and one had a bell around its neck.

Don and his helper picked a small plateau to settle in for a patient wait. They did not want to walk into a camp and surprise anyone, knowing that kind of surprise could cost you your life. Several hours passed before they spotted what looked like two young women moving a few sheep toward the small herd down below them. It would be real trouble if they were spotted spying on these women. Don chose another tactic. He sent his helper back to help bring their flock toward these women and their sheep. If they moved their herd slowly along the river bed, grazing and making normal trail noises it should reduce the chances of alarming the women herders and their sheep. The plan worked. The two herds slowly merged and women's voices could be heard as his men stood in a relaxed manner, two of them even squatting down to appear less threatening. Don could not make out the words, but the conversation was definitely in Spanish and sounded friendly. However, the accent may have been Navajo. This matched his experience with female herders. They were usually Navajo or Hopi Indians, while his Mexican herders were descendants of the Spanish Basque. In the old country, the young boys and old men were the shepherds.

Don gave the herders a chance to get settled before he drove a small number of sheep into the camp. His men had moved along with the other herd until they arrived at the women's camp, which was made up of several huts of sticks and mud. Older women were working the wool with four or five children playing nearby. Don could tell that this was a secure, permanent camp used year after year and the people were definitely Navajo. It didn't take long to learn that this group was part of the Rio Pecos Compound. These women appeared relaxed, which would mean that they had adequate protection, even if there was no visible sign of it. The women's Spanish was very good, even with their Navajo accent. It only took a few hours of casual conversation to learn where the main compound was located.

It was agreed among everyone that one of the younger women would go ahead to the compound so that the guards would be alerted. The Navajos also informed Don that the owner was very strict about new breeds coming into his range.

The compound must be fairly close because four mounted rides arrived the next evening. This was the escort for Don and his men into the

Rio Pecos Compound. The sheep herd would be left in the able hands of the Navajos. The women had been right; the message was to keep the new herd quarantined in this area until they could be inspected.

Although everything seemed on the up and up, Don's fear for himself and his men was real. Being separated from the flock, plus being escorted by mounted armed men could be disastrous. He had mental pictures of their still bodies stretched out in the dry river bed with buzzards gathering overhead. He had taken the risk to save his family; could this be a tragic end?

The rest of the family was holing up in the cliffs of the Canadian River basin way up north. If he was to perish, what would become of his brother and sister-in-law? These thoughts were flashing through his mind; the rising fear level to the panic. The desperation was probably showing on his face when one of the escorts reassured him that the compound was just over the next rise. Good food and cool drinks were only a short distance away.

The compound was practically a village. The central open area or commons was surrounded by adobe buildings, corrals and fencing. Everything was neat and mostly new. But, there were two much older adobe buildings, low and spread out. They were taken toward the biggest and oldest adobe building with its wide covered front porch and hitching rail. Don could smell delicious foods. The aroma of chili, bread and coffee hung in the air. They wolfed down a great meal of home-cooked Mexican food. The bunkhouse they were led to following this meal was another large adobe building, fairly new, but roughly built. They were all assigned a bunk and space to put their things away.

The instructions were clear: Work with the other ranch hands, stay out of trouble, and wait for a meeting with the foreman or owner in a few days. The second day saw hard work repairing corral fences. Then, after the late meal with all hands at the big dining hall, he was summoned to the main ranch house. He was asked to take a seat at a large table with four men. The only question was what circumstances had brought him to the Rio Pecos Compound.

It did not take long for Don Perea's story to be unfolded before the other men. The onlookers seemed interested and understanding, which helped Don to give the details of his family that he had left behind up north.

The leader of the questioners explained the group's role. They would interview newcomers and make a recommendation to the owners as to the newcomers' fitness to join the compound. With approval, an offer would be made to welcome the new members. Any prospective member was then given a complete explanation of the conditions of membership, the costs and benefits. If the visitor did not want to proceed into membership, there would be no hard feelings and the compound people would assist the visitor on with his journeys.

Don was very excited about the prospect of joining this safe place. It was almost like a dream. Now if he could only get the rest of his family here safely. A brief discussion was held in the other room among the four men, then the apparent leader or spokesman for this group returned with a proposal.

The ranch owner was away for a few days, but he had the authority to act when circumstances required speedy action. The protection of Don's family was of most concern. If he was willing, the compound people would send with him an armed guard and wagons to fetch his family pronto. When everyone was safe and secure at Rio Pecos Compound, then Don and his family members could continue the discussion about their joining this collection of people.

Rising before dawn, it took less than an hour for Don to be on his way north. They were taking two wagons, extra horses and five armed guards. Don's shepherds would drive the wagons, then herd the small band of sheep back. The sun was creeping over the eastern mountain range. Its golden rays were knocking a little of the chill off the air. By the time the sun cleared the mountaintop, they had a good two hours of trail behind them. With the fairly lightweight wagons and excellent horses, using the main trail north should cut their travel time by one-third.

They encountered only a few wagons and riders on the trail north. As was the custom, the passing groups would exchange information about the trail, the weather and even sometimes trade supplies. The last leg of the trip took less than a day after they saw the settlers and wagons off to Santa Fe. Don cautioned the guards that he and his shepherds should enter the hideout alone. This plan would allow Don's brother to recognize him and prevent any accidental shootings.

On the trip, Don Perez had learned that a major sheep drive was underway from Rio Pecos to Abilene, Kansas. The drive had probably passed by just east of his hiding place a couple of months earlier.

Chapter 18

Clint caught up with the Rio Pecos herd just as they were coming out of the Raton Pass onto the designated plateau. The combined herds of Ortega and Rio Pecos were stretched out for almost a mile. Sr. Bond's herd could be seen merging from the west on to the grassy plateau. The big east/west wagon trail was covered with sheep almost as far as you could see.

The first task was getting the Navajos started on their way back to their homeland. It had been negotiated over the last few days that the Navajos would take cash now for their sheep. Clint could then take all the sheep to Kansas to sell. The Navajos would travel with wagons only to their stone cliff valley which some of the wagon train guides were beginning to call monument valley. A west-bound large wagon train was on the plateau trail when the sheep herds arrived, so Clint made arrangements for the Navajo wagons and carts to travel with the Durango-bound caravan. The Navajos had more than enough money to buy more sheep when they got back to their native land.

The word from these westbound wagon trains that the Navajos had joined told of the railroad operating from Abilene eastward. The stockyards were being built when the Durango-bound wagon train left Abilene almost three weeks ago. It was agreed among all the interest groups that a team would ride ahead to make necessary arrangements at the Abilene railhead. A few extra riders would go along to serve as messengers between the advance team and the herd.

While the advance team had representatives from all the herds with authority to negotiate a sales price, the Bond ranch foreman would be the key negotiator. He had handled the sales of Sr. Bond's sheep over many years.

The railroad tracks had extended almost two days' ride west of Abilene. Hundreds of workmen, wagons, and stacks of railroad ties were strung out off to one side of the old wagon trail. The finished line looked like a giant, lazy snake stretching out across the Kansas plains. The curves were long and gradual as compared to the wagon trail with its sharp curves and many direction changes. In many places a new supply road for the railroad had replaced the old wagon trail.

They arrived at the railhead midday. The loading ramps were still being built, but many had been completed. A train was being loaded with sheep, cattle and wool when Clint and his group pulled into the stockyards. A few inquiries led them to the main purchasing offices. Only a few small herds had been brought into Abilene so far, but the east was waiting for wool, beef and mutton, and they were willing to pay for early deliveries.

An agreement was reached for the entire herd before late afternoon. Clint was impressed with the bargaining skills of the Bond ranch foreman and the stockyard purchasing agent. Both of these men had successfully completed negotiations like this before and they seemed to enjoy the process. A price of 30 cents per head was agreed upon and it included the 2,000 head that the Basques would be allowed to shear and sell the wool. The wool price was going as high as eight cents per pound and some of the Merino sheep produced two to four pounds per head. The Basques could select the 2,000 head to shear. There was a shearing barn available at the far end of the stockyards. The wool exchange would be completed in the same warehouse.

The two messenger riders were sent back to the herd with the news. They also took some supplies such as sugar, coffee and spices that would be getting low due to the long trail drive. The purchasing agent set up bank drafts for a portion of the estimated head count. The group could then draw on their individual accounts until the final tally for the whole herd was completed. There were seven separate owner groups for the purchasing agent to set up accounts for, with the Rio Pecos herds being only one.

Sr. Bond's foreman led the way to the Abilene bank for everyone to make the first draw, and then immediately to the Longhorn Café for a real beef steak. Everyone in the group had had enough mutton over the last two months. The Bond ranch paid the entire café bill in appreciation for the good drive and the great price the sheep had brought, though it would be almost a week before the final count would be completed and the final bank draws authorized.

In the meantime, everyone would go their separate ways. For his part, Clint had run across an interesting ad in the Abilene newspaper. The

U.S. Government was looking for experienced land surveyors or people that would be willing to take training to become surveyors. An exam was being offered for those with experience. Anyone making adequate scores could qualify for various levels of surveyor certification and the job offers. All interested parties should contact the U.S. Army Field Office at 330 Main Street, Abilene, Kansas, and come prepared for a six-hour written exam and a five-hour field survey.

Clint made easy work of the survey exams. Some six to seven years ago when he was working for that lazy surveyor ramrod, Clint had actually assumed most of the work. During this time, Clint was a little resentful when the chief surveyor took all the credit and, of course, the high pay while Clint did all the work. Those two years of surveying experience had taught him everything that was on the exam and a lot more. Clint's scores were so high that the Army Colonel wanted to put him to work training other surveyors. Clint declined and looked at the newly registered surveyor's license in his hand. The wax seal was still a little wet and shiny. The Army had eventually provided him with his master surveyor's stamp and an offer to report to either the Durango or Santa Fe offices for survey assignments.

For Clint, his next mission was the investigation of Atkinson and Johnson, as to where they got their funds, who was actually calling the shots, and what could be done about the false surveys and claims that Atkinson was filing against his ranch and others in Abilene. Word was circulating around town that a huge sheep herd was about to arrive in three or four days. It was the largest herd to-date to even come to this new railhead. The town buzzed with excitement and money, just the atmosphere for Clint to engage in his favorite pastime – gambling. The liquor was flowing, money was moving from hand to hand and conversation was lively and relaxed. Clint played his usual slow pace of winning small amounts from each table, listening to the stories, and then moving on to the next saloon. By the time the final tally had been made at the stockyard and the bank was ready to make the final payment, Clint had enough information for his next move . . . and a lot of extra cash.

The Basques set up a big camp outside of Abilene. They offered great food and celebration before heading back to Rio Pecos. To no one's surprise, everyone that had participated in the drive agreed to attend. Clint instructed all of his people to meet at the bank to distribute the payment of gold coins according to the final count as previously agreed upon. The payments to Ortega, Bond and other ranches were handled by the Bond foreman. The Ortega shepherds took their pay from the Bond foreman and then joined the Basque clan for the planned return trip to Rio Pecos. Clint made arrangement for his large share of gold to be held by the Abilene bank, and then transferred bank to bank by the U.S. Army payroll run to the Santa Fe bank.

The Basques' feast was certainly an excellent way to celebrate their successful drive and the great sale. It had been a long drive, but it was completed with no major injuries or any loss of animals, and the final price was much more than anyone had counted on or expected. Everyone was ready to head home, so Clint purchased three new wagons that the Basques were to drive back to Rio Pecos fully loaded for the trading post.

St. Louis was Clint's next stop. All the gossip he had heard led through St. Louis, then back east to New York City or Washington, D.C. The finances were coming out of New York City, but the political and lobbying work was apparently being done in the nation's capital. Clint decided to follow the money trail. To grease the wheels in St. Louis, he requested the Abilene bank transfer a sizable amount to a St. Louis bank under the name of the newly licensed surveyor, Clifton M. Martinez. Clint would carry this draft and his personal identification from the Abilene bank for this withdrawal. This Abilene bank did a lot of business with the real estate agency that Atkinson was associated with in St. Louis. The St. Louis Citizens Bank was chosen because it had been used by the Atkinson group. So, Clint had the Abilene Bank set up his new accounts with that particular bank.

The train ride into St. Louis sure was an easy way to travel. The railroad executives had added a dining car, gaming and lounge car for those that would pay a little extra. The money men in the gaming car would more than make up the cost of the trip. It was during some of these games that Clint learned which hotel and the office location Atkinson used in his St. Louis trips.

Clint's visit to the bank in St. Louis to withdraw a rather handsome sum of $20 gold pieces was a little unusual. The teller asked a lot more questions than he had expected, but Clint had all the identification necessary for the withdrawal.

After the teller completed the transaction, he insisted on the name of a hotel or some location where the bank could contact him if necessary. Clint decided to provide this information to the teller, but he had rented two rooms when he first arrived in St. Louis. The first was in the Grand Hotel and was suitable for the master surveyor, Clifton M. Martinez. The second was in a rather rundown, old back-street hotel that would serve as a good place for the Mexican hide-trader with his smelly clothes and shy manners.

The teller accepted the Grand Hotel address without further questions. It seemed to Clint that once he had Clint's room location, the teller had completed his task. Clint then made a hurried trip to his Grand Hotel room to remove any monies, papers and other critical information that he had left there. Then he rearranged the room with great care so he would be able to tell if anyone visited him while he was enjoying the poker games around town.

The next two days were very rewarding as far as the poker playing and finding new information. The days also revealed two or three shadows that seemed to be following Clint from saloon to café to hotel. Also during the second day, in one of the very crowded saloons, Clint felt at least two pickpocket attempts on him. He had not acted like he knew what was happening, but had just moved enough to make the attempts miss.

Gradually Clint learned that there were three men that were trailing him on nearly every move. By the third day this cat-and-mouse routine was getting old and tiresome, until Clint learned that Atkinson was due to arrive at the hotel in the next day or two. Clint decided that those games would continue until Atkinson arrived. A pattern was being created day after day that would keep Clint close enough to the Grand Hotel, but that would be boring for his followers. By the time Atkinson arrived, Clint's shadowers were already slacking off on their close surveillance, but they felt they knew his patterns and could check on him occasionally.

Atkinson's entrance to the hotel was showy and he was certainly catered to, as most big spenders were in this town. One man accompanying Atkinson was Clint's biggest concern. He knew the type – slick, shrewd and vicious. He was apparently Atkinson's personal bodyguard and maybe his hit man. It did not take Clint long to observe at least two knives, a hidden boot gun, a sleeve Dillinger and a Colt 44 in a fast-draw holster. By the way other men steered clear of this bodyguard, Clint knew that his reputation had been earned in a deadly way.

It wasn't long before those following him reported one by one to either the guard or to Atkinson directly. His room was visited and thoroughly searched in a professional way. A normal lodger would never suspect that his room had been searched. Clint kept to his set pattern with regularity with the addition of one new stop. He found an excellent local café on a back street, a few blocks from his old hotel room. The alley from the main street back two blocks to the old café was clearly an ambush waiting to happen. It was Clint's hope that the attack on him would be limited to this alley. It was narrow enough to force them to approach him no more than two at a time side-by-side, or from both ends of the alley. Either way, he would have a split-second to defend himself rather than being shot down from a distance. The alley was also close enough to Main Street that they would probably try to take him with clubs and knives and not bring unwanted attention with gun shots.

Although the fear and adrenaline were pumping through his veins and brain when he saw the ambush developing, there was a silent satisfaction that he had read them accurately and that they were following his plan as if they had read his script. Two men followed Clint into the alley, with a third coming toward him from the opposite direction. They were walking casually until they could get close enough to spring the trap.

The bodyguard, the most dangerous of the three, even spoke a friendly greeting as he neared. The guard was so quick that Clint felt the tremendous impact of a broad blade knife hitting his gut before he could spin around and break the attacker's arm while his hand was still attached to the knife. The spin threw the first attacker into the two men coming from the rear. Clint reached around the screaming first attacker and grabbed the nearest second thug by his long hair. With a swift jerk Clint heard his neck snap. The third man then stabbed Clint in his shoulder before Clint could remove the knife from his gut and rip the throat of the original attacker. Clint could feel the blood running down his back from the fresh shoulder stab. Two men lay dead in the alley dirt and the third was backing away, wishing he had never joined this party. Then,

Clint heard the voice of Atkinson. The third man hesitated only a second, but it gave Clint enough time to grab the man by the throat and drag him down to the ground on top of him. Clint now held the big knife at the belly of the only surviving ambusher. Clint whispered in his ear, "Tell Atkinson that you have the man – and if you don't make it convincing, I will lay you open from top to bottom." Clint released enough of the hold on the man's windpipe for him to call out the message. He could then hear steps coming toward him down the alley. The street light behind the man allowed Clint to see that Atkinson himself had taken his bait. Clint slit the throat of the man lying on top of him then lay there as still as a dead man in an alley with the two other still corpses.

Suddenly, Clint was looking into the face of Atkinson not five feet away when his bullet hit Atkinson square between the eyes. Clint's gun had been drawn quickly and stuck between the arm and body of the man lying on top of him.

Clint quickly escaped down the alley toward his old hidden room. He could hear a crowd gathering on Main Street in response to the shot. Clint needed to get to his room to stop his bleeding and to see how severe his gut stab was. His stomach ached, but did not hurt as much as his shoulder. He rolled around in the dirty alley just before emerging onto the back street. While the dirt might help stop the bleeding, he needed to mask the fine clothes he was wearing. Some blood running down your back, with a cover of alley dust, and no one would even suspect that you were wearing nice clothes.

Clint made it to his room up the back stairs without raising anyone's attention. The shoulder knife cut was deep, but this type of cut would heal quickly if he could stop the bleeding. When Clint removed his jacket and shirt, to his surprise there was no blood on his stomach. His money belt that had been full of $20 coins was split and a nice imprint of a $20 golden eagle was on his stomach. The force of the knife must have driven a coin flat against his gut. It had hurt like the devil, but did not break the skin.

Clint washed out his shoulder wound with whiskey and tied a tight bandage around his chest and over his shoulder. He put on as much pressure as he could stand, then drinking as much water as he could force down, he lay down placing all his weight on the shoulder bandage. His rage and fear and the bleeding had taken all his strength. He was asleep in no time.

The sun was up the next morning before Clint's eyes opened. At first he thought he was okay, but the first movement hurt both his shoulder and his stomach. After a close inspection of his bandages, he was relieved the wounds had bled very little through the night. The bandage and the pressure had done the trick. Now if he could just keep it from opening up again. He needed food, water and more rest.

Carefully, he began to put on the old clothes of the hide-trader, and then eased down the back stairs to the old café. He had rolled up the blood-soaked dress clothes from the night before and dropped them in a waste barrel down the street. It took three full days of eating, sleeping, and resting before Clint started to get his energy back. By the fourth day, Clint went and purchased some new dress clothes and returned to the Grand Hotel as the well-dressed master surveyor. Rumors were all over about poor Mr. Atkinson being killed in an alley not five blocks away from the Grand Hotel. Atkinson had killed two muggers, but had then lost his life. His bodyguard had also been killed in the fray. The killers must have been good because Atkinson's bodyguard had been known in St. Louis to have killed at least 10 men himself over the past few years.

Clint also heard that the railroad detectives were being sent out from New York to help the local U.S. Marshal investigate the killings. Mr. Atkinson had a lot of political and financial connections back east.

Clint needed medical attention for his shoulder stab wound, but seeking it here in St. Louis was too risky. Another option would be to fake an accident and try to get a local doctor to sew up the wound. Clint did not think he could ride far without opening up the big cut. If only he could rest for a couple of weeks, the wound would heal okay, but any riding would start the bleeding again. So, he decided to put on his hide-trader look and seek out a small doctor's office in a poor section of St. Louis. Shortly Clint found a small clinic that was taking walk-in workers, so he got in line.

The clinic's procedure was almost like they were working on cattle. For $1, or whatever you could pay, they run you through a wash-up by an aid, and then the doctor came in and sewed up the cut without even asking how you got injured. The aid then cleaned up the wound and put a tight bandage on it. As soon as you could pay something, you were shown the door. There must have been 20 people waiting to see the doctor when Clint left the clinic. The doctor had been rather rough, but the stitches looked good. They should hold. Clint stopped at a nearby general store to get some wound ointment to protect against soreness.

The next thing was to get some rest. The trains were running from St. Louis to Chicago on a regular schedule and Clint decided to hide out in Chicago for a few weeks. He had plenty of cash and a big city was a good place to get lost. The trip to Chicago turned out to be a good choice. There were so many people aboard that a new face was not even noticed. The other item of interest was that both Colt and Winchester gun makers had manufacturing facilities in the industrial area of Chicago. Colt had just released a new .44 caliber handgun and rifle that used the same cartridge that could be reloaded as needed. Clint made arrangements to buy ten of each with two sets of reloading equipment and a lot of spare parts. They were to be shipped to Santa Fe in care of Mr. Jenson at the Santa Fe bank. Clint also purchased an extra set to carry himself.

After a few weeks of rest, Clint felt like a new man. He bought some very nice clothes and started circulating around the finest restaurants and lounges. It wasn't long before he was invited to join one of the poker games for railroad and business executives. His two-week stay in Chicago gradually turned into a month. The rich businessmen had lots of money and they didn't seem to care about losing it. They just enjoyed the competitive sport and a good challenger. Clint had no trouble in providing both a good line of conversation on western life and top competition. If he kept up this pace of winning, he would make more than his whole herd of sheep paid out.

The only really bad information was related to the railroad company's push westward and the number of forced foreclosure of properties along the proposed railroad right-of-way. The railroad companies were taking a lot of legal actions to acquire the property along the rail lines. The railroad executives were rather open in their discussions around the poker table and at meals about their plans and methods. It seemed fairly common knowledge among these men that the property along the Santa Fe Trail from Raton Pass to Gloriata Pass was being acquired either by foreclosure or being purchased outright. Their primary land purchasing agency was headed by Claude Johnson and Charlie Atkinson out of Las Vegas and Española. Funding was being arranged through Claude Johnson's wife's family as major stockholders. To Clint's surprise, this group of executives seemed to know nothing of Johnson's problems in Española nor Atkinson's recent death in St. Louis. Clint put his name in the mix for possible contacts if they ever needed a master surveyor. He could be located through the Santa Fe banker, Mr. Jenson. Clint let the group know that he was in contact with a lot of the property owners between Las Vegas, Raton Pass and on down to the Gloriata Pass region. If they ever needed a good contact in that area, they should send him a message. With that seed planted for them to ponder, Clint headed back to St. Louis.

Chapter 19

Clint returned to his old room in the St. Louis Grand Hotel without being questioned by anyone. He had arranged to pay for the room a month at a time. A few inquiries reduced his concerns about the Atkinson murder. The U.S. Marshal and the railroad detectives had concluded that it was a mugging; a robbery that went bad with Atkinson and his body guard being killed in the process. A third robber was looked for as an accomplice, but they had turned up nothing in over a month. The hotel clerk told Clint that the U.S. Marshall had tried to contact him several times and when they received word that Clint was in Chicago on business the inquiry had been dropped.

Clint cleaned out his room, paid up all his bills and caught the train to Abilene. It was time to head off the railroad's push to acquire a big section of the Rio Pecos Ranch. A scheme had hatched in Clint's mind during the many discussions he had overhead in Chicago. The railroad executives wanted to buy large tracts of land along the route to develop and sell later. They did not want to deal with a lot of small parcels of land from multiple owners.

So, Clint's scheme would be to deed out the entire route the train should take to individual Rio Pecos Compound families. Then the Rio Pecos

Compound would hold in common the proposed railroad right-of-way.

Clint's survey skills could locate the most desirable route for the rail lines and set that land aside. Then, the land along the right-of-way could be divided up into parcels with individual ownerships. Clint could then offer that strip of right-of-way to the railroad at a bargain price, thus leading the railroad through Rio Pecos Ranch at the most compatible location for the Rio Pecos Compound land owners. It was just a plan; now, to implement it in gradual stages without his true identity being discovered.

Clint loaded his possessions onto the train out of St. Louis and headed back to Abilene. It would be good to pick up his horses in Abilene and hit the trail back to Rio Pecos. He was carrying a new survey instrument that he had bought in Chicago. It would be a real help in laying out the railroad right-of-way and new property lines. It was with some sadness that he was planning to break up the Rio Pecos Ranch into much smaller pieces. The families at the ranch had worked very hard to make a community and one way to ensure its continuation was to share ownership. People respond to ownership and take much greater pride in their own home and land. Clint reasoned with himself that the ranch had been obtained by gambling, sleight of hand and by blackmail.

It was only fair that hardworking, needy families would inherit some of the land. Clint was going to carve out the canyon and stream where he had kept the horses as his hidden place. He would hold onto the original adobe house as his main home if or until his past caught up with him.

His horses were in great shape when he picked them up from the stable in Abilene. They were well-feed and full of energy. The horses were ready to run as soon as he hit the trail, but he had to hold them back. They would need a little conditioning for a few days because they had been in the stable and corrals for almost two months. Being in the open air with good horses under him put joy back into his spirits. His shoulder wound was almost completely healed.

As Clint rode through the Raton Pass onto the grassy plains of the upper Canadian River basin, the cool fall air was starting to color the aspen leaves. The chill was in the air. Some snow was on the mountain peaks and the streams were already ice cold. He headed into Las Vegas to check on the status of land claims and try to find out what Claude Johnson was doing.

Clint went to the land title office first. The only notice on the bulletin board that identified his property was his own counter claim against the Johnson/Atkinson land title challenge. It was past due. When Clint asked the clerk about its status, the clerk took the notice down. He reported that no one had shown up at the hearing so the challenge had been closed. He had just forgotten to remove it from the bulletin board.

The clerk said he had not seen Claude Johnson or Charlie Atkinson for at least two months. Clint reported that he had heard a rumor that Atkinson had been killed in St. Louis. This news caught the clerk by complete surprise. Clint then told the clerk that he was a registered land surveyor and was looking into some of the past surveys in the region for the railroads and government.

Clint spent two days circulating around the Las Vegas cafés and saloons picking up what information he could find. It would appear that Johnson had just about withdrawn from public view. Atkinson and his gunmen had left the area. Most of the rumors had him going back east. By the second day, Clint's rumor about Atkinson's death was coming back to him at the card tables. Clint was a little surprised how quickly and widespread his leaked rumor to the land office clerk had made its way around Las Vegas.

Clint was still in Las Vegas when some freight wagons stopped on their way to Santa Fe. They had some newspapers from St. Louis that told the story about the Atkinson and bodyguard killings. This produced quite a buzz around the town as the facts backed up the rumors. Atkinson had made a big footprint in this area. His men had intimidated most of the ranchers for years and he had been a part of land claims against most of the large land holders. There was a collective sigh of relief when the official news got around that he was dead.

The final leg of his journey back to Rio Pecos went rapidly. It was a feeling of coming home after being off fighting a war. He rested on the high overlook of the Rio Pecos Compound. The village had really taken shape. People were busy working on new buildings. He could see smoke coming out of the blacksmith shop forge and people were walking in and out of the trading post. It truly had become a small town in less than three years. Clint had just started off the bluff toward his ranch house when two of his Mexican guards rode up. They were doing their regular surveillance when Clint had been spotted about an hour earlier. A brief report was given. Everyone had returned safely from the sheep drive to Abilene. While Clint was gone, a family from up above Las Vegas had come to the compound with a small herd of sheep. They were looking to join the Rio Pecos Ranch. Their sheep were being held in a separate area even though everything seemed okay with the new people and their livestock. In fact, one of the men had joined the guard unit and was an excellent rifle shot. The rest of the family had settled into work in the village.

Clint's house was clean and warm. It was good to be home. A visit to the trading post brought him up-to-speed on the happenings of the last few months around Rio Pecos. The restocking of supplies from Abilene had been a real help. The trading post was in good position to get through the winter. One more trading trip was scheduled to the Santa Fe market before bad weather. At least three weddings were in the planning stage. While the parents were in worry mode, the young people were very excited.

The new family of sheepherders from up north seemed real nice and industrious. The Juan Cruz family had finished off two houses for them. The new sheep tenders were working their own herd over on the northwest range, but keeping them separate from the Navajo and Basque herds.

Joe Black had received the three new wagons from Abilene with the extra spare wheels. One of the Kansas boys had become a good helper for Joe Black. He was learning the blacksmith trade and doing a good job. There was getting to be too much work for Joe by himself. It also allowed Joe to spend more time upgrading the guns with the extra gunsmith supplies Clint had sent back from Abilene with the Basque herders.

A visit to Joe Black's shop was impressive. Joe had expanded his forge and added work tables. Clint could see two wagons in the process of being rebuilt to an almost new condition. Joe's helper was busy shoeing two horses and demonstrating almost professional skills. Joe was proud of his student and for good reason. Clint told Joe he had ordered ten new handguns and rifles that used reload cartridges. These new supplies would be in Santa Fe by now. He had also ordered some extra parts that Joe may be able to use in converting some of their existing handguns so they could use the new reload cartridges.

Clint then went out with three of the Mexican guards to look over the horses in the hidden canyon. The guards were reporting that all the horses were broken to ride with the exception of some young colts. All the horses that had made the sheep herd drive returned in good shape. The new horse that Clint had purchased in Abilene had been turned loose in the canyon. The only horses missing from Clint's herd were the mares that had been sent to Albuquerque for breeding. The guards were volunteering to make the trip to bring them back. Clint let them know that a late November to mid-December meeting in Santa Fe with the Spanish land grant holders would be a good time to make the pick-up arrangements. Señors Ortega, Bond and Perez would be holding their annual meeting in Santa Fe before the end of year meeting in Albuquerque with the Spanish land grant lobbyist.

Clint laid praise on the Mexican guards for the excellent condition of the horse herd. The young colts were an excellent crop this year. Clint's horse breed was developing as he had hoped. He was looking forward to adding the strength of the Spanish strain to his herd.

Chapter 20

A full community meeting was called to discuss the last trading trip to Santa Fe before winter and review progress and the future of the Rio Pecos Compound. Each family group or clan went over their needs and items available for trade. Most of the people wanted to make the Santa Fe trip, but enough agreed to stay at the village to maintain everything and to tend the livestock and herds. The Pueblos were making a big haul of specialty clay back to San Juan Pueblo. They also had a lot of top quality pottery to sell on the market square.

The Navajo family had the new blanket designs and jewelry to sell. The Basque families were sending about half their people to trade wool, mutton and blankets, and then purchase their supplies for next year. The rest of the Basques would tend all the sheep left on Rio Pecos Ranch. All the Kansas settlers wanted to make the trip. Even the young blacksmith was looking forward to a holiday in Santa Fe. The Juan Perez family, the newest Rio Pecos arrivals, wanted to stay in their new homes. They had had enough adventure for a time. They would pay their dues by covering for anyone that wanted to make the trip.

The final item of business was the discussion on the railroad's plans to extend their tracks down the Santa Fe Trail, through the Raton Pass, then pass through the western edge of the Rio

Pecos Ranch on through the Gloriata Pass, then head south of Santa Fe down the Rio Grande to Albuquerque. Clint estimated that this section of the rail system would be built in the next ten to fifteen years. He presented his plan to survey out the best rail route and then sell that route at a cheap price to the railroad company. This would help control the location of the railroad right-of-way. The next step was dividing up Rio Pecos Ranch into small sections of land, all fronting on the railroad right-of-way. Ownership would be placed in the names of individuals to have and to hold permanently. This should discourage the railroad land purchasing agents from choosing alternate routes for the rail lines. Clint cited some examples of how the U.S. Congress and some land reformers back east wanted to break up the large land grant holdings. By breaking up this large tract of land into smaller pieces, it might avoid or at least discourage a break-up of the Rio Pecos Compound lands. Clint informed the group that he had obtained a surveyor license from the government and would be working with all the families to plot out the lands and get them recorded in the Santa Fe land title office.

He would also be meeting with some of the large ranch owners in Santa Fe. One proposal that Clint was hoping to work out with these owners was the concept of open range. If all the land owners would agree to large movements of sheep from the colder high mountain pastures all the way to the warmer southern plains toward Tucumcari, it would create an ideal sheep-raising country. Most of the sheep owners at Rio Pecos were very interested. This was the type of sheep ranching the Basques were used to from the old country in Europe. None of Clint's people had ever lived in Spain or other parts of Europe, but their family stories told of those places and times. The Navajo matriarch was not excited about the idea because their tradition had been to stay pretty much in a small area. However, she would not object as long as she was allowed to maintain her own area and continue the traditional living conditions.

The next few weeks were spent preparing for the Santa Fe trading days and putting together the survey documents needed to record the individual land tracks.

Twenty-four individual deeds and surveys were prepared, plus the long strip of land for the proposed railroad right-of-way. Each deed held 1,280 acres or two sections of land with a one-half mile frontage along the proposed railroad right-of-way. The balance of the land Clint held in his own name including the original ranch house, well and stables, plus the almost 3,000 acres in and around the canyon where he was raising and hiding his horses, and all the land east of the Rio Pecos River.

Payment for the land was an agreement to occupy and improve the land for at least five years, allow the free movement of livestock for grazing and trail drives, and to participate in the protection of the Rio Pecos Compound and its people.

The trip into Santa Fe was full of joy, excitement and hope for a good future as new property owners. Some of the families expressed a little concern about their new responsibilities as landowners, but everyone wanted to get started on their land. The Santa Fe land title office accepted all the new deeds when Clint provided his proof of master surveyor certification and U.S. Government identification.

The Rio Pecos camping area at the traders' campsite looked almost like a town in itself. One family moved into the old house in town and watched over the trading goods. After a little cleaning, Clint set himself up in the other house. The Rio Pecos people had agreed on a 10-day trading session on the market square.

Clint set out to make contact with the other ranchers – Bond, Ortega, and Perez. He also needed to find out what Claude Johnson had been up to over the past few months. Sr. Bond was in town for his annual meeting in Santa Fe, plus preparing for his winter visit to Albuquerque and the annual meeting with the Spanish land grant holders. Sr. Bond was all praise for Clint and the successful drive to Abilene. A southern sheep drive was being planned for the upcoming summer to either El Paso or Mexico City. The final details would be worked out at the Albuquerque conference.

Clint was sure Rio Pecos Ranch would have about 50,000 head ready by that time. His Basque herders may not want to go, but he was sure his Mexican guards would make the trip.

Sr. Bond accepted Clint's offer to send two or three of his guards to Albuquerque with him to retrieve Clint's mares if the horse breeding had been successful. Clint then presented Sr. Bond with one of the colt revolvers that he had purchased in Chicago. After that, Sr. Bond would not allow Clint to buy anything: All meals and drinks were on him. The revolver represented the finest workmanship that Sr. Bond had ever seen.

A meeting with Mr. Jenson confirmed that the gold had made its way from Abilene to Clint's account in the Santa Fe bank. The bank was most appreciative of Clint's trust in them. If Clint would agree, the bank would lend out some of Clint's account value and split the profit from interest.

Clint authorized Mr. Jenson to loan out 50% of his gold value to businesses and ranchers in the area. When Clint added a restriction that none of the money could be loaned to the Claude Johnson Ranch or any of its activities, Mr. Jenson said that the railroad detectives and Johnson's men were still investigating the relationship between the Rio Pecos people and the murders in and around Santa Fe. Clint was surprised to learn that Johnson was openly contending that the Rio Pecos people were behind the killings and the burning of his barn. Clint had thought that Claude Johnson had been chastened enough to mind his own business. Clint's St. Louis information that Johnson had almost bankrupted his wife's family should have cut off his funding. A second look would have to be made into Johnson's activities and his source of funding.

The next stop was the Santa Fe railroad office to present his surveyor credentials and the availability of the right-of-way across the Rio Pecos Ranch. He then learned that Claude Johnson's real estate agency out of St. Louis had been paid for other sections of land north of Las Vegas. This was probably the source of Johnson's new money. It was also the same land that was in dispute with Sr. Ortega and his land grant.

Clint asked to see the surveys and titles for the northern railroad right-of-ways. This confirmed that it was the same land that Atkinson had falsified with surveys against Sr. Ortega's land grant holdings. Clint alerted the Santa Fe office that these right-of-ways may be fraudulent, and suggested that the clerk should contact the railroad head office to authorize a new title search and resurvey. All payments to Johnson's real estate agency should be stopped, in Clint's opinion. At the very least, they should withhold any additional payments until the railroad could investigate those land deals more thoroughly.

With his mission complete in Santa Fe, Clint settled into his hobby of gambling. Or put another way, he would help redistribute the wealth of reckless and rich card players. This time Clint played the part of the rich land owner as he dressed in his finest clothes and with the new handguns from Chicago. Clint watched the faces of the other gamblers to see if any spark of recognition ever showed. This clean and well-dressed businessman was a long way from the lowly Mexican hide-trader of last year. Clint was surprised at the number of invites he received to join the big money tables of the rich. This never would have happened to the old hide-trader. Clint enjoyed his deception and the easy money of the rich and foolish. It was on the fourth or fifth day of gambling when Claude Johnson joined the card game. When the introductions went around, Clint made the point that he was a new surveyor that the U.S. Government had certified to help with the railroad right-of-way problems. That information was a shock to Johnson even though his surprise was covered fairly well. Clint enjoyed taking Johnson for a big sum of money that night before Claude excused himself. Clint could see the fire in the man's eyes. This loss of money in front of the Santa Fe businessmen just might push him into drastic action. Clint would have to be increasingly alert. It would be a good idea to gather his guards and put them on alert also. His trading people could also be the target of Johnson's revenge or pure frustration. Clint's pleasure of fleecing Johnson could come back and bite him or his people. After some reflection, Clint wished he had been a bit gentler with Johnson, but he sure did enjoy those few hours of watching him lose hand after hand.

Clint sought out his guards and put them on alert to the possible revenge from Johnson and his men. Clint had his men identify as many of the Johnson gunmen as they could. He helped to point out the ones he had seen either at the ranch or riding with Johnson. Several of the men were the gunmen from the Las Vegas connection to Atkinson. It took two more days of watching to identify about 12 men that seemed to make up the core of Johnson's crew. Clint then put spies to watch the Johnson Ranch and the movements of Johnson and four of his key men. If anything was initiated, Clint should have an early warning from his spies. Clint had recognized about six of the men as the same ones that had tried to rob his supply wagons the year before. It was Clint's best guess that they would try to rob his traders when they headed back to Rio Pecos loaded with supplies and money from their trading on the market square.

Clint had his guards pick up the crate of new guns from the freight office. The shipment had arrived from Abilene the month before. Clint's men took turns learning to reload shells and practicing with the new repeating rifles and revolvers.

The last preparation before the wagons left Santa Fe headed back to Rio Pecos was a change in costumes. Six extra Mexican guard suits were prepared in black and trimmed with silver on saddles, belts and holsters. His Mexican guards were then dressed in work clothes and sent out ahead of time to occupy posts along the trail. The Mexican guards were not happy to put their expensive and showy clothing in their saddlebags, but they went along with the plan. Six of the men from the wagon train were outfitted in the made-up uniforms of the Mexican guards and rode some of Clint's best horses. They would ride close to the wagons. A few of the new rifles would be placed inside the wagons with the best shooters. The Mexican guards in their work cloths would all have the top quality firearms. If the attack was made on the wagon train, Clint's hope was to catch Johnson's men in crossfire between the rifles in the wagons and his guards up on the ridges. Clint's spies reported that Johnson had left the ranch with 14 men. Seven gunmen in two parties had ridden around Santa Fe and were headed toward Gloriata Pass.

Clint had taken three young men with him to a good lookout spot. Each of them had a fast horse and knew how to ride. They were going to be the messengers for this battle, if it came to that.

The wagon train left the Santa Fe traders' camp on schedule as was planned. The first group of Johnson riders was spotted about noon moving along parallel with the Santa Fe Trail just north about one-quarter of a mile.

The first young rider was sent back to the wagon train with this information. Shortly after the first messenger rider had left, the second group of Johnson riders was seen some distance behind the first group. This group of seven was staying on the Santa Fe Trail, but moving very slowly. It was Clint's guess that the ambush would occur about four miles up the trail when the first set of the Johnson riders would be able to pass the wagons and block the trail. This would put the wagon train between the two groups without a way out. The country was very rough, so the wagons would not be able to leave the main trail. Clint sent the second messenger on a fast trip to the wagons hoping he could get through before the rear gang closed the gap with the wagon train. The last messenger moved with Clint as they snuck along the southern rim overlooking the wagon train. It was slow-going in very rocky terrain and heavy underbrush. Clint could tell by their pace that the rear Johnson groups would reach the wagon train before he could get into a position to help from the rim above. He then changed his plan and tore-off down the steep mountain slope to the trail. This put him almost a half-mile behind the Johnson gang. The third messenger was sent on along the rim with instruction to place a few shots toward the Johnson gang when the fighting got started. Assuming that his Mexican guards would be close enough to join the fight from the other end, this would make the ambushers think they were surrounded.

The gunfire started up ahead before Clint was close enough to see the action. He quickly tied a rope across the trail between two big pine trees just about rider height. He then moved toward the fight cautiously, not wanting to walk right into an ambush. Then, he heard a shot from the upper ridge, which would be his young man. The rapid fire of the repeating rifles was very clear now, so the wagon train was putting up a fight. It was less than 20 minutes before he heard three or four horses riding hard down the trail toward him.

The attack must have been broken and some of the Johnson gang was retreating. Clint had moved off the trail behind some big boulders for cover. Four riders came around the curve just above the rope trap at top speed. When they saw the rope, it was almost too late. The front riders tried to stop, but the slower reaction of the rear two caused a huge pile-up with men and horses flying everywhere. Clint called out for the downed gunmen to drop their weapons. Their answer was a hail of bullets toward Clint's hiding place. Clint dropped two of the three standing and this fight was over. The fourth rider had apparently been killed in the pile-up.

The shooting had stopped coming from the wagons. Clint tied up the lone surviving gunman. All four horses seemed to be okay, so Clint led them up the trail toward the wagon train. By the time Clint reached the wagons, everything was under the control of his Mexican guards. Two of Clint's people had been killed and several people had minor wounds. The guards had two of the gang tied up with minor wounds. All the rest of Johnson's gunmen had been killed.

Two of the horses that were pulling the wagons had been hit during the gun fight. One was dead and the other had to be put down. All the Johnson gang horses were rounded up. Roadside graves were dug for the dead. Markers were placed for the two Rio Pecos people giving names and dates. The grave markers for the Johnson gang just said, "Here lie 11 bandits who killed 2 Rio Pecos people." The final ride into Rio Pecos Compound was somber as everyone mourned the loss of their two friends. The killing of so many people, even in defense, was very painful and a waste of human life.

The three captured robbers were released with a message to Claude Johnson that he was next to account for his bad deeds and his plotting against the Rio Pecos people.

Chapter 21

A month had passed since the shootout with the Johnson gang. The Rio Pecos wounded were healing very rapidly. The whole village was putting the final touches on the last of the new houses and preparing for the winter months. Clint was headed back to Santa Fe with two of the Mexican guards. The guards would go with Sr. Bond to Albuquerque to bring back the mares that had been bred with the Spanish stallions.

Clint was following up on the activities of Claude Johnson, plus having a little fun gambling. The first café stop for a good beef steak uncovered the story that Mr. Johnson had taken the stage back east to meet with the railroad executives in St. Louis. He had just left the day before with an overnight layover in Las Vegas. If Clint left immediately with one extra horse, he should be able to reach Abilene about the time Claude would be arriving by stage. The word was that Claude was traveling with two professional gun hands as bodyguards. The waitress at the café was very descriptive of the guards and their dress. They had intimidated several of her best customers. She described them as strutting around like peacocks in their fancy clothes and expensive double-holster Colt revolvers. Both guards were identically dressed and armed. They could be brothers or maybe close kin. One of them went by the name of Jake Tilson. She had never heard the other name. They had openly bragged about getting even with the Rio Pecos people for bushwhacking the Johnson Ranch workers. The story these two Johnson guards were spreading had the Rio Pecos people squatting on Mr. Johnson's land, and saying that the Rio Pecos people bushwhacked the Johnson riders when they tried to serve notice on the compound. Mr. Johnson was going to have the U.S. Army evict the Rio Pecos people off the railroad right-of-way and his property. The rumor had it that Claude Johnson and his family had a lot of financial power back east in both New York City and the national capital.

Clint traded one of his horses with one of the Mexican guards so he had the two best horses to make the run to Abilene. A quick pack job at his old town house and he started. If his calculations were good, he should be able to pass Johnson's stagecoach almost a full day before he got to Abilene to catch the train. Train schedules were uncertain, but Clint's goal was to beat Johnson to St. Louis.

Clint was more than a day's ride out of Abilene when he overtook the stage at a rest stop for a team change. He rode clear of the stage's horse changing station and continued on to Abilene.

Clint's first stop in Abilene was the train ticket office. A train was leaving late that evening for St. Louis. This gave Clint enough time to check in with the U.S. Army survey office and railroad office to verify that they had received his offer to sell his right-of-way through Rio Pecos Ranch. Neither office had seen the papers, but both were very interested. The Colonel remembered Clint and his excellent showing on the survey exams. He was glad that Clint had agreed to work on the railroad right-of-way issue between Raton Pass and Santa Fe.

The death of Atkinson had left a lot of the land surveys incomplete. The Santa Fe land title clerk had sent a message last month that the Atkinson/ Johnson land deals may be improper. The Colonel had sent word to the St. Louis office to withhold all further payments until the legal issues could be checked out.

The Colonel was aware that Claude Johnson was headed to St. Louis or even further east to free up his money and persuade the railroad company to complete the land purchases from him. Johnson was claiming to be the sole owner of the jointly held lands upon the death of Atkinson last summer in St. Louis.

Timing could not have been worse. The stage with Johnson and his two guards arrived before the train left Abilene headed to St. Louis. Clint's horses were being moved around in the stockyard next to the rail station when Johnson and his men walked by. Clint had boarded the train a little earlier and could see Johnson's reaction when he spotted Clint's horses. Clint watched Johnson go back to the ticket office. Clint was beginning to feel trapped. He did not think of Johnson as a gunman, but those two guards with Johnson's help would be more than Clint could handle by himself. Clint's idea had been to select his time and place in the big city of St. Louis. Abilene was much too small and he was well recognized in this town. But being trapped inside a railcar was almost certain death, so he snuck out the rear side of the train and headed to a public place. He selected the biggest saloon and eased himself into a card game. He chose a rear table back against the wall. If he was to have any chance, he had to keep Johnson's guards in front of him. It did not take long before one of Johnson's men walked through the saloon. When he spotted Clint, he left immediately. The return of all three was predictable.

Johnson sent one of his gun hands over to join Clint's card game. It only took a few hands for the quality card skills of the Johnson gunman to appear. Clint was an expert gambler himself and this guy was very close in his handling of that deck of cards. Clint was watching the cards so closely that he almost missed the movement of the other gunman, toward the wall near Clint, just off to his side about four or five feet.

When another player left the table, Johnson joined the game. Clint was face-to-face across the table with two men that wanted him dead and a third just off to his left that would gladly help them accomplish that deed. Johnson's gun hand was making obvious cheating moves with the cards. Clint knew it was to sucker him into challenging, and then being killed by all three guns. The whole shootout would be called a gambling dispute and dismissed.

Clint had taken the precaution of having two guns in his lap so he did not have to draw a gun while seated. One of the other players finally got fed up with the cheating and stood up to protest. This was the moment that the Johnson team was waiting for and Clint knew it. Clint fired two shots at once from under the table. Johnson and his card playing partner were thrown back as their guns exploded into the floor. The standing card player had partially blocked the line of sight for the last gunman. The gunman had put a bullet into the challenging card player. Clint had tipped his chair over backward and put two shots into the last standing gunman just as he was pulling off another shot. Clint felt the burn of a bullet in his leg. The standing gambler fell onto Clint in obvious pain. His gun fell right beside Clint. With a quick motion, Clint used the other man's gun and put another shot into each of Johnson's men and Johnson himself. Clint was looking directly into the helpless eyes of Johnson when that fatal bullet struck him.

Once the shooting had stopped and the smoke had cleared, the local law officer and doctor were sent for. Clint's leg wound was not serious, but the other card player had taken a rather bad shot into the upper chest and shoulder. He had lost a lot of blood, but the doctor was sure he could pull the man through

The story was very clear to the law officer. Johnson's guard was cheating at cards. When he was challenged, the shooting started. The challenger had killed Johnson and the cheating gunman. The second guard had then shot the challenging card player and Clint in the leg. Clint had then shot the guard in self-defense. This story was confirmed when the law officer inspected everyone's guns for empty shells. Clint had reloaded with the exception of two empty shells. There had been so much confusion following the shootout that no one noticed Clint reloading both guns. The wounded card player did not remember all the shooting, but accepted the conclusion that he had killed the cheating card player and the cheater's boss. In fact, he accepted the role of hero quite willingly and with pride. The two other players confirmed the dead gunman's card cheating and put the praise on their fellow card player for challenging the cheater. Clint was seen as an innocent bystander that had defended himself. The demise of Claude Johnson could not have been planned better than this accidental encounter. The word got around that one of the dead gunmen was known as Jake Tilson, a well-known professional guard for the Atkinson/Johnson enterprises. He was credited with almost a dozen killings from Chicago, St. Louis and as far south as New Orleans. Everyone was telling Clint and the wounded card player how lucky they were to have survived the gun battle. By now, the saloon shootout had grown to a new level of heroism, having Trent Jones, the wounded card player, standing up against three gunmen and killing them all even though he had suffered a serious gunshot wound to his upper chest and right shoulder, his shooting arm. It was a miracle that he was able to continue shooting after he had fallen. Trent Jones was an overnight celebrity.

Clint could only smile to himself and reinforce the myth every chance he got. His wound was mending without infection and his job was done. He hung around Abilene for a week to see that Trent Jones was recovering okay and that no new details were uncovered to challenge the myth of the saloon gun battle.

Clint had another mission now that the threat of land claims against Rio Pecos Ranch had died with Atkinson and Claude Johnson. Joe Black had given Clint the name of his sister and her two young sons that Joe had heard were living in Chicago. She had escaped slavery in the Deep South while the Civil War was raging. Joe did not know what had happened to her husband. The only clue was that Joe had placed his sister at one of the meatpacking plants on the south side of Chicago. Joe had asked Clint to get a message to her if he got back to Chicago. Joe had found a safe place to live and JoAnn Jackson was welcome to join him. Her two boys went by the names of Fred and Andy. They were about 10 and 12 years old.

Clint set off on the train ride to Chicago with hope for the future and a sense of pride that even Joe Black felt safe at Rio Pecos Compound.

The End

About the Author

William F. Martin was born on a Kentucky farm and moved west in the mid-sixties on an assignment with the federal government's program to help Native Americans. His assignment to Santa Fe, New Mexico, began a lifetime love affair with the American West. His writing interest was developed with the publishing of many technical journal articles and textbooks on environmental and engineering issues. He obtained a B.S. degree in Civil Engineering from the University of Kentucky and a M.S. degree in Environmental Engineering from the University of Texas.

After assignments in South Dakota, Arizona, and Texas, he has lived near the Gulf of Mexico on Treasure Island, Florida, and in the Blue Ridge Mountains in Boone, North Carolina.